Goddess Girls

PERSEPHONE
THE
GRATEFUL

READ ALL THE BOOKS IN THE GODDESS GIRLS SERIES!

ATHENA THE BRAIN

PERSEPHONE THE PHONY

APHRODITE THE BEAUTY

ARTEMIS THE BRAVE

ATHENA THE WISE

APHRODITE THE DIVA

ARTEMIS THE LOYAL

MEDUSA THE MEAN

GODDESS GIRLS SUPER SPECIAL:
THE GIRL GAMES

PANDORA THE CURIOUS

PHEME THE GOSSIP

PERSEPHONE THE DARING

CASSANDRA THE LUCKY

ATHENA THE PROUD

IRIS THE COLORFUL

APHRODITE THE FAIR

MEDUSA THE RICH

AMPHITRITE THE BUBBLY

HESTIA THE INVISIBLE

ECHO THE COPYCAT

CALLIOPE THE MUSE

PALLAS THE PAL

NYX THE MYSTERIOUS

MEDEA THE ENCHANTRESS

EOS THE LIGHTHEARTED

CLOTHO THE FATE

PERSEPHONE THE GRATEFUL

Goddess Girls

PERSEPHONE
THE
GRATEFUL

JOAN HOLUB & SUZANNE WILLIAMS

Aladdin

NEW YORK   LONDON   TORONTO   SYDNEY   NEW DELHI

ALADDIN

An imprint of Simon & Schuster Children's Publishing Division

1230 Avenue of the Americas, New York, New York 10020

First Aladdin hardcover edition December 2020

Text copyright © 2020 by Joan Holub and Suzanne Williams

Jacket illustration copyright © 2020 by Glen Hanson

Also available in an Aladdin paperback edition.

All rights reserved, including the right of reproduction in whole or in part in any form.

ALADDIN and related logo are registered trademarks of Simon & Schuster, Inc.

For information about special discounts for bulk purchases, please contact

Simon & Schuster Special Sales at 1-866-506-1949 or business@simonandschuster.com.

The Simon & Schuster Speakers Bureau can bring authors to your live event.

For more information or to book an event contact the Simon & Schuster Speakers Bureau at 1-866-248-3049 or visit our website at www.simonspeakers.com.

Jacket designed by Tiara Iandiorio

Interior designed by Hilary Zarycky

The text of this book was set in Baskerville.

Manufactured in the United States of America 1020 FFG

2 4 6 8 10 9 7 5 3 1

Library of Congress Control Number 2020937981

ISBN 978-1-5344-5740-9 (hc)

ISBN 978-1-5344-5739-3 (pbk)

ISBN 978-1-5344-5741-6 (eBook)

CONTENTS

1   MINTHE   *Page 1*

2   LATE!   *Page 19*

3   THE COMPETITION   *Page 29*

4   TEAMMATES   *Page 38*

5   DISAPPOINTMENT   *Page 65*

6   THE FIRST CLUE   *Page 84*

7   PIRITHOUS PROBLEMS   *Page 95*

8   THE WHITE BLACKBIRD   *Page 108*

9   CLUE TWO   *Page 127*

10   THE LAST TWO CLUES   *Page 144*

11   THE CHAIR OF FORGETFULNESS
Page 178

12   TO THE RESCUE!   *Page 199*

13   MEALTIME AT MOA   *Page 222*

We appreciate our mega-amazing readers!

Kiah D., Gabby A., Valeria C., Hannah B., Melody S., Zoey R., McKenna W., Emeline D., Hannah D., Ashleigh D. and Rebecca D., Layla S., Shannon Y., Descendre S., Sabrina P., Evie and Luna P., Autumn A., Camren N. and Zellah C., the Andrade Family, Kendra P., Lorelai M., Aubrey N. and Top N., Ellis T., Kira L. and Christina L., Christine D.-H., Olive Jean D. and Eli Reuben D., Malia C. and Olivia C., Kati B., Alex S., Stephanie T., Isabella R., Nadia N., Julia T., Amelia B., Olivia M., Sarah M., Danielle H., Endreya B., Ryzelle S., Kyzara S., Emily N., Sloane G., Jeremy G., Izzy F., Mackynzie C., Lori F., Caitlin R. and Hannah R., Antonia W., Deni D., Kiaya M. & Leila M., Vivian D.A., Lana W., Zoya B. and Katya B., Kathy P., Lynn P., Shannon O., Catherine O., Julie H., Paul H., Kristen S., Saad S., Barbara E., Emily S., Sara L., Bonnie W., Grace W., and you!

—J. H. and S. W.

1

Minthe

PERSEPHONE'S GREEN EYES SPARKLED WITH excitement, and her long red hair blew this way and that as breezes rushed past her. She was in the mood for an adventure, even if there was only time enough for a small one.

"Let's go to a part of the Underworld I haven't been to yet," she suggested to the godboy Hades as they sailed down through a large crack in the Earth.

She was seated behind him on the back of his black stallion. "Maybe someplace with unusual plants?" she went on. "Since we have a few hours to kill, I mean." As the goddessgirl of spring and growing things, she was fascinated by plants of all kinds.

Like her, Hades was a student at Mount Olympus Academy, where Zeus, King of the Gods and Ruler of the Heavens, was principal. Though Hades was only fourteen years old, just a year older than her, he ruled the realm of the Underworld.

It was Thursday morning, so normally Persephone and Hades would be in classes right now. However, today MOA students had the whole morning free while teachers at the Academy took time to plan lessons. This meant that the two of them didn't have to be back at Mount Olympus until after lunch.

Hades turned to look at Persephone over one

shoulder. They were each other's crushes, and though he was sometimes dark and brooding, she thought he was super cute with his long, curly black hair, flashing dark eyes, and fine straight nose.

"Works for me," he replied, raising his voice to be heard over the wind as they flew ever downward and deeper below the earth. "Minthe has been asking me to stop by. You could come with."

"Who's Minthe? Girl or boy?" Persephone asked. She didn't remember Hades ever mentioning the name before.

"Girl. A naiad. She's caretaker of the River Cocytus," Hades informed her. Naiads were water nymphs that inhabited rivers, springs, and waterfalls. Or even wells and fountains. Anything with fresh water, actually. The Cocytus was one of five rivers that flowed through the Underworld. There were *always* interesting plants to be found growing near rivers.

"Sure, I'll go with you," she replied. She'd only ever been to one of the five rivers in the Underworld before, the one called the Styx. It was the one that the newly dead from Earth crossed to get into the Underworld, ferried there by a crusty old ferryboat captain named Charon.

"Okay. *Hot*," said Hades. He grinned over his shoulder at her. "I've decided to substitute that word for 'cool.' Because the Underworld is actually hot, but in a cool way. Get it?"

Persephone grinned back. "Got it." Located deep below the Earth, the Underworld was a creepy, dark, lonely, smelly place mostly, but she had grown to love many things about this realm that Hades loved so well.

The two of them had first become truly acquainted in a cemetery, of all places! She'd been relaxing among the gravestones, weaving a daisy chain, when—not more than twenty feet away from her—Hades had burst up through the ground on his black stallion. This guy had been all frowns and troubles back then, but their friendship had made him much happier. Her, too, for that matter!

Just now, Persephone swayed sideways as Hades pulled on his horse's reins to change the direction they were traveling. The black stallion veered left. Below them, she could make out various features of the Underworld that had become (much to her surprise) endearingly familiar to her by now. Like the misty, marshy entrance near the spot where Charon's ferryboat docked. And the immense fields of white-blossomed asphodel. Their roots were the main food of the shades, human souls that lived in that part of the Underworld.

Far off in the distance she caught a glimpse of a dark hole in the ground and shivered, quickly looking away. It was the entrance to the deep pit of Tartarus—the awfulest, ickiest part of the Underworld. Only the truly evil wound up being sent down there. Not a place she liked visiting, that was for sure!

"There's the Cocytus," Hades said, pointing downward. Persephone studied the river as they rode lower and closer to it. Its waters, dark with mud, moved so sluggishly that they appeared to be almost completely still. As the stallion took them nearer, a rotten-egg smell made Persephone wrinkle her nose. *Sulfur. Yuck.* The stinky smell, ever present in much of the Underworld, didn't bother her as much as it used to (and it *never* bothered Hades). However, here it was particularly strong.

Suddenly two large, ugly vultures with hunched

shoulders and sharp, curved beaks flapped past. They clawed at each other, making raspy, hissing sounds as they fought over the right to land on one particular blackened and gnarled tree on the riverbank. From the branches of other hideous and misshapen trees along the river's edge, the whiny, mournful cries of screech owls drifted upward. Looking at this forlorn spot, Persephone doubted she'd find any plants to interest her. Oh well.

The black stallion landed them on the riverbank with a gentle thump. Hades slid from the horse's back and then gallantly helped Persephone hop down too. Standing on the bank, she stared through a layer of sulfurous fog into the depths of the foul and lifeless River Cocytus.

"Ew," she murmured, coughing and cupping a hand over her nose. "What kind of nymph could possibly stand to live in this yucky place?"

"Um . . . me?" said a sarcastic voice. Persephone gasped and glanced around. Slowly, a beautiful girl about her age materialized out of the mist. She was standing in the shallows of the river before them, a foot or two from its bank. The girl was slender, with long, gorgeous moss-green hair. She wore a filmy white gown that, though pretty, seemed just a little too big for her. Its hem was damp and swirled around her ankles in the watery sludge. *(Um, ick!)*

However, she and the part of her dress above the river's waters had magically become dry and sludge-free the moment she rose from it. Persephone wished this girl hadn't overheard her "yucky place" comment, but she obviously had.

"Hey, Minthe. What's up? I got a message that you wanted to see me?" said Hades. He looked quizzically from her to the river as though trying to figure out if there was some sort of trouble here that he needed to take care of.

Clasping her hands together at her waist, the nymph smiled warmly at him. "I'm so happy you came!" she gushed. "But who's this?" she asked. She extended a hand with ballerina-like grace in Persephone's direction, accidentally flinging drops of muddy brown water toward her.

At least Persephone *assumed* it was an accident. She took a step backward to avoid being splashed by the muddy water. For a fraction of a second, she thought she saw a malicious look flash across the beautiful nymph's face. But then the girl sent a fake-looking smile her way.

"I'm Persephone," Persephone said quickly. "And you're Minthe? Nice to meet you."

Minthe crossed her arms and nodded, shooting her a long up-and-down look that wasn't exactly welcoming. "I've read about you in *Teen Scrollazine*," she said at last, referring to the news-scroll that was mega-popular with practically everyone of school age in Greece (and beyond). "You're the goddessgirl of spring and growing things, right?"

Whether Minthe approved or disapproved of her and her goddessgirl title, Persephone couldn't tell. "That's right," Persephone replied, nodding and offering her a friendly smile. "Hades was just telling me that you, um, live here and take care of this river?"

"That's right." Minthe stuck out her chin as if daring Persephone to comment again on the dismal state of the River Cocytus. Which she never would have done to begin with if she'd known that Minthe would overhear her, of course. Everyone at MOA knew how much she didn't like hurting others' feelings!

Persephone's eyes flicked to Hades, hoping he'd say something to ease this uncomfortable conversation. However, he had temporarily tuned them out and was busy talking softly to his stallion while leading him over to nibble some grass on the riverbank. Ordinary grass, by the looks of it. Certainly not a plant to excite her interest, unfortunately.

"Cute chiton," Minthe commented, her eyes running over Persephone's salmon-colored dress. She didn't normally wear pink, but Aphrodite, whose favorite color was pink, had convinced her that the color suited her. And she'd been pleased to discover it really did.

"Thanks. I got it from the Immortal Marketplace on a shopping trip with my goddessgirl friend

Aphrodite last weekend. Do you know it? The IM? It's located halfway between Mount Olympus and Earth. Lots of immortals hang out there."

"Nope. Must be nice, though," Minthe muttered. "Unlike you, nymphs like me are only considered *minor* goddesses. We aren't free to wander where we choose. I have to make do with hand-me-downs from shades."

So that's why her gown doesn't fit quite right, thought Persephone. To her ear, this nymph sounded kind of bitter and maybe a little angry about her life here. Yet she didn't seem to be trying to improve it. At all.

Glancing over at Hades, Minthe caught his eye. She swayed gently side to side, causing the hem of her gown to disturb the sludge around her again. With a coy smile she said to him, "Not that I'm complaining. If I weren't in the Underworld, I'd never get to see you." She let out a breathy little laugh.

"You *could* visit my river a little more often, though."

Persephone raised her eyebrows. Was this girl flirting with Hades? Sure sounded like it. She felt a flicker of annoyance. But if Minthe *was* flirting, Hades didn't seem to notice. There was a touch of impatience in his voice as he asked, "So, was there a particular reason you wanted to see me today? Some problem?"

"Just wanted to chat and hang out a little," Minthe replied sulkily. "It gets lonely here sometimes, with only the vultures and screech owls for company."

Persephone's annoyance instantly morphed into sympathy. *She* certainly wouldn't want to be bound to this ooky river. Or to any one location, for that matter. Students at MOA were pretty much allowed to roam as they pleased, as long as they attended classes and kept their grades up.

A flash of irritation passed over Hades' face, but then

he pushed back a lock of dark hair that had fallen over one eye, and sighed. "Sorry. I'll try to come by more often. It's just that I usually have a lot to do, and—"

"Oh, I totally understand," interrupted Minthe. "Your job here in the Underworld is so much more important than mine. It's a big realm and full of troublemakers. Plus you've got your studies at Mount Olympus Academy." She smiled wistfully. "That's a place I'd give anything to see."

Persephone shared a look with Hades. Minthe seemed to be angling for an invitation from him to visit MOA.

He shrugged, shifted from one foot to the other, and stared at a dragonfly flitting along the surface of the river. A strange-looking fish poked its spiky head up and gobbled it down before sinking again. *Glub, glub.*

"Sorry, Minthe. I can't take you there," he finally told her. "Only Zeus can issue invitations to visit the Academy."

"Oh, I get it, no problem. So you'll ask Zeus about it, then?" she enthused. "Thank you so much!"

"Um . . . ," Hades mumbled, sounding uncomfortable. Somehow she'd managed to twist his words to try to manipulate him into doing something he'd had no intention of doing.

When he gave no reply, Minthe glanced over at Persephone. "I read in the scrollazine that you're BFFs with Aphrodite and Artemis. And with Zeus's daughter Athena, too, right? And you all go to MOA and live in the girls' dorm there together?"

Persephone nodded. "Um-hmm." She didn't tell Minthe that she'd actually gotten one detail wrong. Persephone didn't live in the girls' dorm, but off campus with her mom, Demeter. Still, she did do sleepovers in the dorm from time to time, especially on the weekends.

"Lucky you. MOA must be sooo cool," Minthe said mournfully. Wow, this girl just kept on hinting, despite what Hades had explained about Zeus being the only one who could invite her to the Academy.

Hades cleared his throat. "We, uh, better get going, Minthe. Nice seeing you, though."

"You'll come again soon?" Minthe responded in a pleading tone of voice.

"If I can," Hades promised. "But maybe you should try to make some other friends around here in the meantime. Maybe talk to some of the shades?"

"Oh, what a good idea! You're so smart," said Minthe, clapping her hands.

Huh? Is she being sarcastic? Persephone wondered.

There was no hint of sarcasm in the nymph's voice. Still, surely Minthe must've thought of befriending other Underworld residents before. *She must only be trying to stroke Hades' ego,* Persephone decided. But he didn't seem to get that. She wished he would. Then maybe he'd speak up and just crush this nymph's crush right now!

Moments later, he and Persephone mounted the black stallion and soared into the air. "Phew," said Hades when they were some distance away. "Minthe's a sweet girl, but she can be kind of *needy* sometimes."

"Sweet?" Persephone echoed as they flew higher. "Uh, yeah, I guess."

She'd hardly use "sweet" to describe the nymph. The words "pushy" and "annoying" seemed like a better fit. She would have been ashamed to admit it aloud, but she was glad Hades had some negative feelings about the beautiful girl.

She did feel a bit sorry for Minthe too, though. She hadn't thought about it in a while, but she and Hades and their friends were actually really lucky to get to attend MOA and travel wherever they liked. She and her BFFs—Athena, Aphrodite, and Artemis—had even gone to Egypt once all by themselves! That was another way she had it better than Minthe. She had friends. Great ones. Minthe was all alone. Hades was right to suggest that she try to make friends in the Underworld, but making new friends could be hard.

Sometimes Persephone forgot to appreciate just how lucky she was. Right then and there, she vowed to be more grateful for all that she had.

2

Late!

*P*ING! PING! PING!

Back at MOA Persephone hurried to her locker, grabbed her scrollbag, and slammed the locker door shut. The warning lyrebell for the start of fifth period was pinging, which meant she'd already missed both lunch and her fourth-period Garden-ology class and only had a few minutes left to get to Science-ology on time. She and Hades had returned later than expected, because as they were leaving the River Cocytus, Hypnos and Thanatos—Hades' two helpers in the Underworld—had flagged them down.

Trouble had broken out at the marshy entrance to the Underworld after some shades got into an argument over (of all things!) which of them had the stinkiest feet. Both claimed theirs were stinkiest, as if that were a *good* thing. And as if stinky feet could ever compete with all the other stinky smells in the Underworld! Anyway, she and Hades had had to make a slight detour so that he could go calm things down. He was allowed to miss classes whenever trouble called him to the Underworld. Since she'd been with him, her absence would be excused too. Still, she didn't like being late.

As Persephone raced along the hallway to class, she accidentally swung her cloth scrollbag a little too hard. Its handle ripped loose on one side; then it slipped from her arm and hit the floor. *Thunk.*

"Godness!" she yelped as several textscrolls tumbled out of her bag and began to roll across the floor.

A beefy-looking godboy named Kydoimos and his godboy pal, Makhai, had been walking toward her on the other side of the hallway. They were deep in conversation and didn't notice the rolling textscrolls until it was too late.

"Godsamighty!" Kydoimos yelled as both boys tripped over the scrolls. Kydoimos banged into the lockers and Makhai sprawled onto the floor, squashing Persephone's cream-colored textscroll flat. She groaned. Of course that *would* be the one for Science-ology.

"Oops! Sorry!" Persephone told them, rushing

over. As other students streamed around her and the boys, she quickly retrieved her scrolls before anyone else could trip, and hurriedly stuffed them back into her bag. Luckily, the two boys seemed unhurt as they scrambled to their feet.

Instead of accepting her apology, however, Kydoimos and Makhai, who had well-earned reputations as meanies (if not *bullies*), glared at Persephone. "Klutz!" Kydoimos spat out. His eyes went to the sandals she wore, and his lip curled. "Muddy feet. Guess you've been down in the Underworld with your stinky boyfriend, Hades?" He leaned toward her and sniffed. "Yep, smells like Underworld to me. Humph. You and your smelly flowers, and him and his rotten, sulfur-reeking Underworld! What a pair!"

Persephone frowned at Kydoimos. Insulting *her* was one thing, but why bring her crush into this?

Then she remembered Hades telling her that these boys had bullied him even *before* she'd gotten to know him.

Now Makhai leaned close to her too and took a couple of loud, huge, comical sniffs. Staring at her dress, he wrinkled his nose. "Ew! What color is that chiton you're wearing? Let me guess—stinky pink?" Makhai always went along with (and even copied!) everything his friend said or did. Laughing, he high-fived Kydoimos.

Startled by the nastiness of their responses, for a moment Persephone just stared at them. Maybe she did stink? At least her sandals might! After all, while Hades had dealt with the feuding shades, she'd stood around in the marshy entrance to the Underworld, which reeked of rotting plants and stagnant water. And she'd also been on the banks of Minthe's stinky river and had droplets of muddy water flung at her!

She automatically bent her head to sniff her salmon-colored chiton in case more than just her sandals stank, but stopped herself in time. These boys never would have let her live that action down!

Embarrassment fueled hot anger through her veins. Persephone drew herself up, then pretended to sniff the air around both boys. "Speaking of bad smells," she retorted, "have you guys got a skunk in your scrollbags or something? Because you don't exactly smell like roses right now. And I should know, since I'm in charge of flowers and stuff. Take a shower once in a while, why don't you?" With that she strode off, clutching her scrollbag to her chest.

When she dared to glance over her shoulder a few seconds later, both boys still stood in the hallway. They appeared to be sniffing their armpits worriedly. With a triumphant feeling, she took off.

She made a quick pit stop in the restroom, where she washed off her sandals in the mosaic-patterned fountain that stood in the middle of it. Afterward, she scrubbed her hands in one of the golden basins and checked her hair in the gold-framed oval mirror above it. Satisfied that that all was in order now, she gave her mirror image a curt, businesslike nod. Then she hurried the rest of the way to class, where she non-stinkily sailed in through the Science-ology room door.

By the time Persephone took a seat, her earlier anger had nearly cooled. It was only then that she felt a bit of remorse for what she'd said to Kydoimos and Makhai. Truthfully, her insult had been kind of lame. Unlike the two boys, she hadn't had much practice insulting people. She was normally nice, but even she couldn't help being angry at their mean remarks. Still, she wished she hadn't responded the way she had. It made her as bad as them! Next time she'd try harder to keep her temper under control and take the high road.

Just then a boy wearing a lion-skin cape with jaws that fit his head like a helmet sat down next to her. "Hi, Heracles," she said. One of the few mortals to attend Mount Olympus Academy, he was her friend Athena's crush, and the strongest boy at MOA.

"Hey." He carried a big, heavy, knobby club with him everywhere he went, and now he swung it from his shoulder and leaned it up against his chair. She'd tried to lift it once. No way! That thing was heavy. However, to him its weight was like a bag of feathers.

A huge godboy named Atlas appeared in the doorway. "Heracles! Save me a seat!" With that the godboy bounded over, his every step causing the floor to shake violently, as if an earthquake were happening. *BOOM! BOOM! BOOM!* The only Titan godboy at MOA, he was Heracles' roommate in the boys' dorm on the fifth floor of the school and, like him, was a champion weight lifter.

All that shaking caused Heracles' club to topple and fall toward Persephone's sandaled feet. She tried to move out of the way, but she wasn't fast enough. As the club landed on the floor, its handle grazed her big toe. *THONK!*

"Ow!" she yelped. For the second time in minutes, anger coursed through her. That stupid club. It was dangerous! Heracles should leave it in his room. It wasn't like he'd need it in class or anything. And Atlas shouldn't stomp around like he did either. She was about to scold them both, but the horrified looks on their faces stopped her.

Anger could lead to more anger, she knew. Just because Kydoimos and Makhai had primed her angry feelings, she shouldn't take those feelings out on others. Heracles and Atlas probably felt terrible about what had happened. The same way *she* would feel if she'd hurt one of them. With that thought, her anger melted away.

"You okay?" Heracles asked her, his dark brown eyes full of concern.

"Sorry, Persephone! My fault!" Atlas cried out, hovering over her.

Persephone rubbed her big toe. "S'okay. I'm fine," she told them, hoping they hadn't sensed her initial angry thoughts. Remembering her vow to be grateful for what she had—in this case, a sore toe, not a broken one—she added kindly, "Accidents happen."

3

The Competition

PING! PING! PING! **THE FINAL LYREBELL RANG TO**
signal the start of fifth period. Persephone and her
classmates snapped to attention as their Science-
ology teacher, Muse Urania, crossed to the front of
the classroom. Her long, curly brown hair was held
back by a midnight-blue headband that glittered with
stars—fitting, since she was a well-respected ama-
teur astronomer in addition to being a teacher. After

placing a lesson planscroll on top of her desk, she turned to face the students.

"Today we will begin a *natural* Science-ology unit," she announced. "And to make it fun, we'll kick it off by learning about various botanical, zoological, and geographic phenomena of Greece through a team competition, to be held tomorrow."

An excited murmur ran through the classroom. Students at MOA, Persephone included, loved competitions of all kinds. Competitiveness came naturally to most immortals. And as the goddessgirl of spring and growing things, Persephone already knew a lot about botany since it involved the study of plants. Her knowledge would no doubt be a big help to whichever team she ended up on.

"Ooh! Ooh!" A lizard-tailed godboy named Ascalabus (Asca for short) raised his hand. He had black hair with a natural green stripe that matched the color of his lizard tail. "How many members to a team?" he asked without being called on. "And can we choose our teammates?"

Muse Urania smiled at him. "I'll get to that. But first let me explain how the competition will work. You'll be going *geo-dashing*. Can anyone guess from this term the nature of the competition?" She paused.

Persephone raised her hand. When Muse Urania called on her, she said, "'Geo' means 'earth,' and everyone knows what 'dash' means. So we'll be rushing around the Earth for some reason?"

"Exactly," said Muse Urania. "In this competition, teams will dash from one place to another in search of a plant, an animal, or a geological formation. A sort of scientific treasure hunt! When you've found what you're looking for in each location, consider this: Sometimes we see what we want or expect to see instead of what is there."

Huh? What was *that* supposed to mean? Persephone wondered. But before she could ask, Muse Urania went on. "The first team to successfully follow the clues and find and visit all four locations wins."

From the left side of the room another hand shot up. "Will there be a prize?" asked Iris, the goddess-girl of rainbows. Her small, sparkly pink wings gave a flutter as she spoke. Cute as her wings were, they weren't strong enough to actually fly her anywhere. But she didn't need them for transportation, because she could create rainbow slides to get wherever she wanted to go!

Muse Urania smiled brightly as Iris's long wavy hair, turquoise at first, slowly shifted through all the colors of the rainbow. "Isn't learning something new enough of a prize?" she asked the class.

Hmm. Persephone thought about that. She *did* love to learn new things. But Muse Urania had called this a competition. Didn't competitions usually involve prizes?

"Just kidding," said their teacher, as low-level grumbling began to sweep the room. "I hope you all *prize* learning, but yes, there will also be more traditional prizes. At that, spirits lifted, and enthusiastic murmurs replaced the grumbles.

"Like what?" Atlas blurted out.

Muse Urania beamed at the class. "Members of the winning team will all get trophies."

This brought cheers, and more questions, too. "How big?" Atlas wanted to know. "I'll need to make room."

No doubt he already had an entire closetful of trophies after winning so many wrestling championships, thought Persephone. Despite having once won a laurel crown in the long-jump competition at the Girls' Olympic Games, and ribbons at various gardening competitions, she'd never, ever gotten a trophy. It would be *hot* (to borrow a term from Hades) to win one!

"Yeah, and are they silver or gold?" a voice called out from the back of the room. It was a student named Hylaeus. He was a centaur, so his upper body was that of a boy and his lower body that of a four-legged horse. Since it was nearly impossible for him to sit in a chair, he always stood at the back of the classroom.

"Will the trophies have our names?" asked Heracles.

Boys! Honestly. A trophy was a trophy, thought Persephone. Who cared what metal it was made of, how big it was, or if their names were engraved on them? She'd be super *grateful* to earn one, no matter what!

By the time Persephone tuned in again, Muse Urania had answered everyone's questions. Now she was explaining that the two sections of her Science-ology classes—which she taught third and fifth periods—would combine for the competition. "Teams will be randomly made up from a mix of both classes," she told them. "Since there are twenty students in my third-period class and fifteen of you in this one, I've decided to divide you into seven teams of five members each," she added.

"Same number and size of teams as in the Temple Games!" Persephone exclaimed.

Muse Urania blinked. "Yes, I suppose so."

The annual Temple Games were a very big deal. The weeklong contest of skill, strength, and strategy featured competitors not only from MOA, but also from other realms, such as the Undersea, and many places outside Greece. Persephone had participated earlier in the year, but not on one of the teams. Instead she and Aphrodite had helped Principal Zeus and his nine-headed office assistant, Ms. Hydra, organize and conduct the games.

Persephone loved being of help to others like that. *Hmm,* she thought. Maybe Muse Urania could use some assistance organizing this geo-dashing competition. She was about to raise her hand to ask, when another thought occurred to her. Volunteering might disqualify her from participating on a team, like it had in the Temple Games, because she'd be privy to information that team members weren't supposed to know in advance. This time she'd really like to be on a team. Which would give her a chance at winning a trophy!

Just then, Muse Urania announced that her third-period students would be joining them soon, at the end of class time, to draw names for each five-member team. Persephone straightened as a thrill of excited possibility zipped through her. Hades was in third-period Science-ology. So was her brainy friend Athena. With luck, she would wind up on a team with one or both of them. Woo-hoo!

4

Teammates

I'VE PUT ALL YOUR NAMES ON SLIPS OF PAPYRUS inside this bowl," Muse Urania announced to the thirty-five Science-ology students crowded together in the classroom at the very end of fifth period. She held up a beautiful, black-glazed ceramic bowl for all to see. It was decorated with reddish-orange silhouettes engaged in an archery contest.

Persephone had exchanged smiles and waves

with Athena and Hades as they'd filed into the room a few minutes ago. Now those two and others from third period stood or leaned along the walls, since there weren't enough desks for two classes' worth of kids.

Pandora, a super-curious student with bangs shaped like question marks, leaned over and whispered to Persephone. "Think Mr. Phintias made the bowl?" Though Pandora was in third-period Scienceology with Athena (who was also her roommate), she'd somehow managed to snag an empty desk next to Persephone's. Like Heracles, Pandora was one of the handful of special mortals who attended MOA.

Nodding, Persephone whispered back to the girl. "Probably. It looks like the kind of work he does."

Mr. Phintias was MOA's Crafts-ology teacher and a true artist. Many of the stunningly beautiful vases, urns, pots, and bowls that lined the shelves in his classroom were ones he'd created himself. A lot of them were decorated with reddish-orange silhouettes on glazed black backgrounds and depicted the amazing feats of the gods and goddesses of Mount Olympus.

As the students watched, Muse Urania quickly pulled five slips of papyrus from the bowl. "Here are the names for Team One," she announced. "Athena, Iris, Heracles, Ares, and Kydoimos."

Persephone hadn't realized she'd been holding her breath, but now she released it. *Phew!* Being on a team with Athena would have been great, but she wouldn't have relished having to work with Kydoimos. He and Ares were sometime friends, however, so maybe Ares could keep him in line. After all, Ares was the godboy of war (as well as Aphrodite's crush), so he knew something about troop team-work. Which could help them in this competition.

Just then, she saw Athena lean out from the wall to send Heracles a delighted little wave. Since he was Athena's crush, she was obviously really happy he would be on her team.

It wasn't until Muse Urania drew the names for Team Four that Persephone finally heard her own name called. "Poseidon, Persephone . . ." She crossed her fingers while she listened intently for the names of her last three teammates. "Antheia, Makhai, and Hades."

Hooray! She did a fist pump. She and her crush would get to be teammates! Twisting toward her, Hades flashed her a smile and a thumbs-up, which she returned wholeheartedly. She wished Makhai weren't on their team, but at least he wasn't quite as awful as his friend Kydoimos. In fact, without Kydoimos around to give him mean ideas, Makhai might prove to be an okay guy. She could hope, anyway. And she really liked Antheia. She was the goddessgirl of flowering wreaths, so they had in common a love of plants. Poseidon, godboy of the sea, was pretty cool too, most of the time.

"So that you can all participate in tomorrow's geo-dashing, Principal Zeus will excuse you from your usual Friday classes," Muse Urania announced once all seven teams had been named. "Meet me here in the morning at eight o'clock sharp for your instructions." She grinned at them. "And remember, if you don't want to annoy your teammates, don't be late!"

There was scattered laughter at this. Persephone, who had once been voted by mortals in a *Teen Scrollazine* poll as Most Dependable, knew there was no chance *she* would be late. Although she'd been late to school today, that had been for a very good reason, *and* unavoidable. To not show up on time for something as important and exciting as this assignment, she'd have to be at death's door. And since she was immortal, that would never happen!

Moments later, Muse Urania excused everyone. As students started filing out of the classroom into the hallway, Persephone caught up to Hades. She'd hoped they could walk and talk together, but just then Muse Urania called out, "Poseidon and Hades, may I please speak with the two of you for a few minutes?"

"Sure," both godboys answered at the same time.

Hades twisted his head back toward Persephone. "No idea what it's about," he said in a voice too quiet for their teacher to hear. "See you later, okay?"

Persephone swallowed her disappointment. *Okay,*

she mouthed back. It was only after she'd exited the classroom that she remembered she had Goddessgirl Squad cheer-team practice that afternoon. But she'd see Hades at dinner, and hopefully they could talk about a good geo-dashing strategy for tomorrow. Go, Team Four!

She made her way through the halls to the Academy's marble staircase and climbed to the girls' dorm on the fourth floor, one floor below the boys' dorm. Aphrodite was already wearing her blue-and-gold cheer-team outfit when Persephone entered the room they shared whenever Persephone stayed the night at the Academy instead of going home.

Like most of the dorm rooms, theirs had two beds, two closets, and two built-in desks. Aphrodite had painted pink and red hearts all over their room's walls and draped sparkly red fabric above the bed she slept in. (The other bed was for Persephone.) Persephone knew exactly where she'd put her trophy if her team won. Front and center on the middle shelf over the desk at the end of her bed.

Hmm. She'd already decorated that shelf with gifts from friends and other knickknacks. There was, for example, a stuffed knitted owl Athena had given her for her birthday last year, and a ceramic vase Aphrodite had made for her in Crafts-ology class. (Because Persephone was the goddessgirl of spring and growing things, Aphrodite had painted a border of flowers all around the vase.)

There wasn't a lot of space left on the shelf, Persephone noticed. Now she sort of wished she'd listened when Muse Urania was answering the boys' questions about the trophy's size. She hoped that if she won one, it would fit!

"Hey, kitty, kitty," Persephone called softly, spotting a ball of black-and-white fur on top of one of the six puffy, heart-shaped pillows that were arranged just so on Aphrodite's neatly made bed. Adonis, the kitten they shared, jumped off the pillow, ran over to Persephone, and rubbed himself against her legs.

Meow, meow, meow.

She picked him up. "Are you looking for a liddle cuddle-wuddle, kitty-witty?" she cooed as she petted his soft fur.

Meow, meow, meow.

Aphrodite grinned and gave her long golden hair a flip. Then she grabbed her pom-poms from the top shelf of her perfectly organized closet and made up a cheer on the spot, performing stylish movements to go with it:

"Hip hip hooray,

Persephone's here!

Now we can all

Get going to cheer.

Two, four, six, eight!

Hurry and dress, girl,

Or we'll be late!"

Persephone laughed. "I'll be fast." She gently set Adonis on top of Aphrodite's plush red velvet comforter, which was stitched with a pattern of little white hearts. He promptly padded over to the heart-shaped pillow he'd only just left, curled up on it, and began to lick his paws.

Persephone moved to the closet at the foot of the bed that was hers whenever she slept over. Aphrodite had cleared a bit of space for her—not easy for the goddessgirl to do, because she had dozens and dozens of outfits and sometimes changed them four or five times a day! Luckily, Artemis, who roomed next door, let Aphrodite store some of her overflow clothes in *her* unused spare closet. Artemis had no roommate, only three dogs. And they didn't *need* closet space.

After opening the closet, Persephone pulled her cheer uniform from its hanger. Though she'd mostly put Minthe out of her mind since she and Hades had returned from the Underworld, her concern that the naiad was crushing on him suddenly pushed its way into her head again, like a sprout poking up through soil. While she changed into her uniform, it occurred to her that she could ask Aphrodite for advice on what, if anything, she should do about Minthe. After all, Aphrodite was the goddessgirl of love (and beauty, too), as evidenced by all the hearts decorating her side of the room. She was an *expert* on this sort of thing!

On the other hand, Persephone wasn't sure how much she wanted to reveal about her "problem." She was a private kind of person, which meant that she didn't always feel comfortable discussing personal stuff. Even with friends. Still, she could really use Aphrodite's advice.

She shifted her eyes toward her friend, who had flopped down on her bed to pet Adonis while waiting for Persephone to be ready. "If you thought someone was crushing on your crush, what would you do about it?" she asked in a casual tone.

Aphrodite sat up fast, her blue eyes wide with alarm. "Someone's crushing on Ares? Who? What have you heard?"

"No! No one's crushing on him. Calm down," said Persephone, giggling a little at her friend's reaction.

Aphrodite sank back down among her pillows.

"Okay, well, that's a relief. But I'm guessing this isn't a general question?" Petting Adonis again, she arched an eyebrow at Persephone. "Out with it. Who's crushing on Hades?"

Persephone dropped her head back and sighed toward the ceiling. Then, while getting on with getting ready, she came clean and told Aphrodite all about Minthe, repeating what that beautiful nymph had said and how she'd acted around Hades. "Hades doesn't seem to like her back," she hastened to add. "He did call her a 'sweet girl,' but then he said that she could be kind of needy sometimes. And I could tell he wasn't happy about that."

"Hmm," said Aphrodite. "So it appears to be a one-sided crush." On her lap now, Adonis purred loudly and flopped on his back so she could stroke his black-and-white belly. Although not all cats liked belly rubs, Adonis adored them.

Persephone nodded as she hung up the salmon-colored chiton she'd been wearing till now.

"Then I wouldn't worry," Aphrodite said. "Without any encouragement, she'll give up on Hades after a while."

"You're sure?" asked Persephone. Aphrodite's response surprised her. Especially since her friend could become quite jealous if she thought anyone was flirting with *her* crush. (Note her earlier reaction!) Not that long ago, she'd actually cast a spell on a goddessgirl named Eos who she'd suspected of crushing on Ares. The spell had made Eos fall in love with *bugs*!

As Persephone began digging around in their

closet for her pom-poms, she recalled how sorry Aphrodite had been to discover she'd been completely wrong about Eos's feelings toward Ares. (And vice versa!) So maybe that experience had tempered her jealousy, at least somewhat?

As if she'd guessed what Persephone had been thinking, Aphrodite said jokingly, "Well, I'm mostly sure. Hard to say definitely, since I don't know Minthe. If I'm wrong, you can always cast a spell on her and turn her into . . . um . . . a *plant* or something."

"Ha-ha," said Persephone, finding and grabbing her pom-poms at last. She was quite certain she would never do anything of the sort. She was not a jealous person.

Purr. Purr. Their kitten's loud rumble made her remember a time when she and Aphrodite had been *super* jealous of each other's attentions to Adonis, though. They'd even argued over who would own him till Principal Zeus got them to share. So, okay. She was not *usually* a jealous person, Persephone silently corrected.

"C'mon, let's get going," said Aphrodite, standing now that they were both in uniform.

As they headed into the hall, Persephone wished she could rid herself of her jealous feelings altogether, but she simply couldn't help herself when it came to Minthe. The best she could do, she decided, would be to not let them get out of hand. Because then she might *act* on those feelings. So, in addition to her vow to be more grateful, she now made a second vow. From now on, whenever jealous feelings arose in her, she would try to curb them.

Right then, Artemis and Athena, who were also on the cheer squad, came out of their rooms. Joining together, the four girls went off to practice on the Academy's sports fields. First they stretched out, and then they did some simple cartwheels and handsprings before moving on to routines and stunts.

During practice, Persephone was pleased when she aced a toe touch, which was basically a side-straddle air split with pom-poms punched outward at shoulder height. It was possible she was feeling a bit too confident when they got to thigh stands, though. As Artemis and Athena stood next to each other in a lunge pose, Persephone hopped up to brace one foot each on their angled thighs, raising her poms in a high V. At least, that was how the move was *supposed* to go. Instead she caught her foot on Artemis's thigh, lost her balance, and sprawled onto the ground.

"You okay?" Aphrodite asked as all three of her BFFs looked down at her with concern.

Persephone wiggled her ankle in a circle, relieved to note that she hadn't sprained or strained it. Then she leaped to her feet. "All good." With an embarrassed grin, she added, "Maybe Kydoimos was right though. I *am* a klutz!"

"Huh?" chorused Athena and Aphrodite.

"What are you talking about?" Artemis asked at the same time.

Persephone explained what had happened on her way to Science-ology class earlier that afternoon—how the handle of her scrollbag had torn, causing her textscrolls to roll out. And how Kydoimos and Makhai had tripped over them and then basically insulted her and Hades.

"You are *not* a klutz," Athena assured her.

"That kind of thing could happen to anyone," Aphrodite added.

"Yeah," echoed Artemis. "Why would you believe anything those boys say? They're just name-calling bullies."

"Thanks, you guys. You're the best," said Persephone. Bumping hips with Athena, she also sent smiles of gratitude toward Aphrodite and Artemis. She could always count on her friends to defend her. Which was definitely something to be grateful for!

Remembering what she'd said to the boys in response, however, she admitted, "I wasn't very nice to them, either, though." Cringing a little, she told her friends what she'd said to Kydoimos and Makhai in the heat of anger, and how she'd caught them sniffing their armpits after she'd stalked off.

At that, her BFFs dissolved in laughter. "That's just *too* funny!" Artemis roared.

"Can't you picture it?" giggled Athena, elbowing Aphrodite.

"Yes, I can! And I love it!" Aphrodite replied. Persephone's BFFs laughed so hard they wound up rolling on the ground. Persephone couldn't help joining in. Thinking back on it, she really could see the humor in the story.

When the four goddessgirls finally managed to get their giggles under control, Aphrodite gave Persephone a quick one-armed hug. "You shouldn't feel bad," she told her. "Those boys deserved to be scolded back."

"Yeah," echoed Artemis and Athena, nodding.

Persephone shrugged. She still believed she could've handled the situation better. Being mean was really never worth it in the end. She always wound up feeling guilty and worried she'd hurt others' feelings.

Toward evening the girls finally climbed the granite steps to the Academy's bronze front doors, their talk moving on to the topic of the geo-dashing competition. "It sounds like so much fun. I wish I was taking Science-ology," Aphrodite remarked after Persephone and Athena described how the competition was going to work.

"Me too," said Artemis. "Apollo will get to play, that lucky dog. He takes Science-ology third period." Apollo was Artemis's twin brother. Although they weren't identical, they did look a lot alike, with their glossy black hair and dark eyes.

Persephone nodded. "I forget which team he's on, but I saw him during the meeting." As the girls entered the Academy and then started up the marble staircase to their fourth-floor dorm, she turned toward Athena. "Sorry you got stuck with Kydoimos on your team," she said.

"S'okay," Athena replied. "I imagine Ares and Heracles will be able to keep him in line. Makhai's on your team, though, huh?"

Persephone sighed. "Yeah. I'm glad he and Kydoimos are on different teams, at least. Without Kydoimos to egg him on, Makhai might not be so awful."

"I bet you're right," said Athena. "Makhai does seem to follow Kydoimos's lead—like he's some kind of sidekick. Maybe it'll be good for him to have to do a little teamwork and make decisions for himself without Kydoimos around."

After changing out of their cheer uniforms, the girls met up again and headed downstairs to the MOA cafeteria for dinner. While eating her nectaroni, celestial salad, and ambrosia pudding, Persephone kept glancing over to the table of boys where Hades usually sat, but he never showed up. Maybe he'd had to return to the Underworld to take care of some new problem? Wait! Could Minthe have made up some kind of crisis to lure Hades back to the River Cocytus? *Humph.* She wouldn't put it past the nymph to do something like that!

Persephone's stomach began to tighten with jealousy. But then she remembered vow number two—to curb those kinds of feelings. Taking a deep breath, she mentally pushed them away.

Though Hades probably *was* in the Underworld, there could be any number of reasons he'd been called there, she reminded herself as she took a sip from her carton of nectar. Maybe those stinky-feet shades were quarreling again, for example. Yes, it was sometimes annoying that Hades wasn't around as much as she'd like because of his godboy duties. Still, she could be grateful for the time he *did* have to hang out with her, right? Right. Thinking this way immediately made her feel a bit better.

When she glanced over at Hades' usual table one last time, she noticed that Poseidon wasn't eating dinner there either. Which meant he might be somewhere with Hades. She also noticed two boys, seated side by side at their table, who she was pretty sure were not MOA students. One was a boy with dreadlocks. She recognized him from somewhere. Oh yeah! From that class trip they'd taken a while back to an amusement park on the island of Crete, just south of Greece.

Leaning over to Athena, she pointed to the boy

and asked, "Isn't that Heracles' cousin Theseus—the one he brought on our class trip to King Minos's aMAZEment Park? Did Zeus invite him here?"

"Yup," Athena replied as she twirled some nectaroni noodles around her fork. "My dad gave him and his friend permission to visit Heracles for a couple of days. So they've been hanging around the boys' dorm all afternoon."

Suddenly the other non-MOA boy sitting beside Theseus jumped up from his seat. Long blond hair flying, he leaped onto the table. Cutlery, plates, and glasses clattered loudly as he began to act out a fight scene, thrusting and swishing a fork (aka a pretend sword) here and there. "Take that! And that!" he yelled with each thrust.

"Who's he?" Artemis asked, squinting at the boy.

Athena rolled her eyes and giggled. "Pirithous.

Some friend of Theseus's. You wouldn't guess it from the way he's acting right now, but according to Heracles, who heard it from Theseus, the guy's a genius. Especially when it comes to technical gadgets and stuff."

Huh, thought Persephone. She really *wouldn't* have guessed that from the boy's antics. Then again, before she and other students at MOA had really gotten to know Hades, they'd all had him pegged as a "bad boy." Most students (except for the ones who had bullied him) had tried to steer clear of him. It just went to show how easy it was to misjudge someone until you got to know them better. Because now she knew Hades was awesome! Most other students agreed. And, unfortunately, one nymph did too. *No!* she reminded herself again. She would not let jealousy in.

A while later, the girls finished their meals and

took their trays to the tray return. "Bye! I'm off to meet my mom," Persephone called to her friends as she hurried toward the cafeteria door.

Unfortunately, she couldn't wait around for Hades to get back from wherever he was. In a few minutes her mom was picking her up in her chariot to fly home. Too bad. Besides wanting to spend time with him, she was bursting with curiosity about what Muse Urania had wanted to talk to him and Poseidon about after class that afternoon. Looked like she'd just have to wait to find out till tomorrow morning when their team met to begin geo-dashing.

After exiting the cafeteria, she headed for the bronze doors at MOA's entrance and then raced down the granite steps to the courtyard below.

5

Disappointment

"HAVE A GOOD DAY!" DEMETER CALLED TO Persephone when she dropped her off at school the next morning. Afterward her mom took off in her horse-drawn chariot for the Immortal Market, where she owned and managed a florist shop called Demeter's Daisies, Daffodils, and Floral Delights. Sometimes when things were really busy, Persephone got to help out working there.

It turned out that Persephone was the first member of her team to arrive at the Science-ology classroom that Friday. She was even better than on time—she was early! And this was despite the fact that she'd had the longest commute of all her classmates, since she didn't live in the dorm full-time. Score!

She nodded at Muse Urania, who was carrying a box full of some kind of identical gadgets to set on her desk. Scroll-gadgets, she realized after a moment. They'd used some of those during the Temple Games to get clues about places to go and to receive important messages from Zeus. These looked like fancier, more updated versions, though. Shiny and white, they were sleeker and slimmer than the Temple Games scroll-gadgets had been.

Like the dependable person she was, Persephone had come prepared for the day's adventure. Before leaving home, she'd counted out some pomegranola bars and thrown them and some apples into her backpack. Soon after she took a seat, other students began to arrive. When Hades finally came in the door, she stood, smiling brightly and waving to him. "Yoo-hoo! Over here!" she called in his direction.

He flipped his long, dark, wavy hair out of his eyes, but he didn't return her smile as he came toward her.

"Hey, why so gloomy?" she asked as he sat down at the desk next to hers. "More stinky-feet shade trouble? When you weren't at dinner yesterday, I guessed you must have had to make an unexpected trip to the Underworld or something."

Hades rubbed the back of his neck. "No trouble in the Underworld," he told her. "In fact everything's calm there for once."

"Then cheer up, grumpy guy," said Persephone. "This competition is going to be fun!" Grinning with enthusiasm, she nudged his shoulder with hers. "Before I forget. What did Muse Urania want to see you and Poseidon about after class yesterday?" she asked.

An anxious look flashed across Hades' face.

Uh-oh, thought Persephone. Maybe it was something bad. Something he'd rather not share. Like a failing grade on an assignment or quiz. "Of course, if you'd rather not say what it was about, that's fine," she said quickly. "It's really none of my business."

Hades opened his mouth to respond, but before he could get a word out, Poseidon entered the classroom, trident clasped in one hand. "Dude!" he called out to Hades, raising his trident. It looked somewhat like a pitchfork, only way cooler. "Did you get your geo-location clue set up?"

Hades nodded. "Yeah. You?"

Poseidon gave him a thumbs-up, then ambled over to Muse Urania and began to speak to her about something.

Looking at Hades, Persephone tilted her head in confusion. "Geo-location clue?"

Hades sighed. "Muse Urania asked Poseidon and me if it would be okay to include the realms of the sea and the Underworld in today's competition. I wasn't sure I wanted people traipsing around in the Underworld, but she was pretty persuasive. So last night Poseidon and I each wrote up a clue for teams to find something in a certain location in each of our realms. Muse Urania did the other two clues to make four in all."

"How exciting!" Persephone exclaimed, wiggling happy fingers at him. Then an *un*happy thought occurred to her, and she abruptly stilled her fingers. "So it won't be a problem that you're on the same team? On *our* team? Could give us an unfair advantage, since you'll know where—"

"Exactly," Hades interrupted. "And that means Poseidon and I aren't on your team anymore. We won't be on any team. Our clues are our only contributions."

"Oh!" Persephone couldn't help feeling disappointed. She'd really been looking forward to her and Hades geo-dashing off together.

Hades seemed to guess how she was feeling. He almost always could. It was one of the many things she liked about him. He took her hand and squeezed it gently. "I'm sorry. I wanted to play on your team too. But just like it was an honor when you helped set up the Temple Games, it's been my honor to take part in planning this competition."

"Right. S'okay," she said, though it really wasn't. "Hey! Maybe I could help too. I could ask Muse Urania if we could go spruce up the Underworld a little before teams arrive. Someone else could take my place on Team Four."

Hades cocked his head at her and frowned. "'Spruce up the Underworld'? What's wrong with it the way it already is?"

"Oh, not a thing," Persephone said quickly. For a moment she'd forgotten that Hades never seemed to notice the smells in the Underworld that made others wrinkle their noses. Things like stagnant water and sulfur, which Kydoimos and Makhai had obviously smelled on her sandals yesterday. And she couldn't remember the last time she and Hades had given his three-headed dog, Cerberus, a bath. He was kind of smelly too. Then she thought of something else. "Wait, if you and Poseidon can't be on our team, we'll be two members short."

Poseidon appeared at their side right then, twirling his trident over his head like a baton. "No, you won't. Muse Urania said we should each choose someone to take our place. When we mentioned it in the dorm last night, Heracles volunteered his cousin Theseus and Theseus's friend Pirithous as substitutes. Those guys are mega-excited at the idea."

"But they're not MOA students," Persephone pointed out. "They're only visiting." She didn't have anything against the two boys, but if *she'd* been able to choose, she would've asked Aphrodite and Artemis to sub for Hades and Poseidon. Having two of her BFFs as substitutes on her team would've been much more fun. Too late now, though.

"It's okay," said Poseidon, misunderstanding her concern. "I checked with Muse Urania when I came in. She's fine with Theseus and Pirithous joining in, even though they don't go to MOA."

Hades gave her hand another squeeze. "I'm sure they'll be good team players," he said reassuringly. "They'll want to prove they're up to the task of subbing for Poseidon and me."

Once again, he'd guessed what she was feeling. He'd understood that she hadn't been worried Muse Urania wouldn't approve of the two boys as replacements. No. She'd been objecting to the *choice* of the two boys.

"Yes, of course. I'm sure they'll fit right in," she

said graciously, to make up for not wanting the two mortal boys on her team. "I've heard Pirithous is really smart about tech stuff, so he could be a big help if we run into problems with our scroll-gadgets."

Some of Hades' friends wandered over, drawing his attention away from her. Shortly afterward, Antheia entered the room. "Ooh! This is going to be so much fun!" she squealed excitedly as she came up to Persephone. The goddessgirl clasped her hands in delight and bounced on her toes, causing the cute fern-and-berry wreath that sat atop her straight brown hair to tilt sideways. She always wore an adorable circlet of some sort on her head.

While Antheia was telling Persephone how happy she was that they were teammates, Hades broke away from his guy friends. "Good luck with the competition!" he called to Persephone. Facing her, he walked backward a half dozen or so steps. Then he wheeled around as he and Poseidon went over to Muse Urania.

"Huh? Where are they going?" Antheia asked Persephone in confusion.

Persephone explained about the change in team members just as Heracles ushered Team Four's two newest members into the classroom. "There they are," she added, pointing the two boys out to Antheia. "Theseus is the one with dreadlocks. Pirithous has the long blond hair."

"Whoa. They're *cute!*" cooed Antheia.

Are they? Persephone hadn't noticed. She supposed they kind of were, though in her eyes no one could be cuter than Hades. She wasn't the only one who saw how special he was. In the same *Teen Scrollazine* poll that had voted her Most Dependable, mortals had voted him Most Fascinating godboy. She agreed with that for sure, though their personalities were pretty much opposite. He was gloomy darkness, like fall and winter, while she was mostly bright and happy, like spring and summer. Yet somehow they clicked.

Heracles brought Theseus and Pirithous over to where Persephone and Antheia were standing, introduced them, and then left to join his own team. As the four introduced themselves to one another, Pirithous kept staring at Persephone.

What? Did I accidentally get lip gloss on my teeth or something? she wondered uncomfortably.

Soon Muse Urania announced that it was time to begin.

"Are we missing someone?" Theseus asked quietly, glancing around the room. "All the other teams have *five* members. We only have four."

"Makhai's not here," said Persephone. Although

annoyed at his lateness, she also felt relieved. If he didn't show up, she wouldn't have to deal with him and his sometimes horrid behavior. She could ask Artemis or Aphrodite to fill in!

"Maybe he's sick?" Antheia suggested. She pointed across the room to where Team One was assembled. "Kydoimos is here. He and Makhai are buds, so he might know what's up with Makhai. Want me to go ask?"

Before Persephone could answer, Makhai burst into the classroom, his hair sticking up in all directions. Muse Urania had just begun to explain that the teams would be using "new and improved" scroll-gadgets, modeled after the devices Zeus had invented for the Temple Games not long ago. After pausing briefly to frown at Makhai, the teacher showed off the scroll-gadget she held.

"These newer devices will allow you to get both text and audio clues about the plants, animals, and geographic features you'll all be searching for," she told them. "But unlike the earlier devices you used in the Temple Games, these can't be used for direct communication. So neither Zeus nor I will be breaking in with instructions." She paused to smile at them. "You'll be fine without our help, though. Learning how to use the devices won't be hard. They're pretty intuitive."

As she spoke, Poseidon and Hades began to circulate around the room to pass out the gleaming white pocket-size scroll-gadgets. "By the way," Muse Urania said, motioning toward the two boys, "there's been a change in the membership of Team Four. Poseidon and Hades will assist me with clues and other things, as you will be visiting their realms, plus two other places during the competition." After a moment's pause she added, "And no, you may *not* ask them to reveal what they know."

There was a smattering of laughter at this.

Persephone exchanged a smile with Hades as he handed her a scroll-gadget. There was one device for each student. Some tried to unroll them right away, hoping to get a head start on figuring out how to use them, no doubt. Noticing, Muse Urania smiled and said, "Your gadgets are magically locked. You won't be able use them until I give you the go-ahead."

"If I had enough time, I bet I could figure out a way to break that lock," Persephone heard Pirithous murmur to Theseus.

"Yeah, probably," Theseus replied in a low voice. "But that wouldn't be fair. Let's just wait and start at the same time as everyone else."

Had Pirithous seriously been thinking of cheating? No way. *That would ruin the fun of winning!* thought Persephone. She was glad Theseus had advised him against it.

"Your geo-dashing will take you to four surprising and interesting locations," Muse Urania went on. "Some of them may be difficult to find or navigate to. Although you will not be allowed to use chariots to travel—other classes are using them today—you may use winged sandals. The first team to return here with proof of having visited all four places wins the competition."

"Proof?" Ares echoed.

"What kind of proof?" Athena called out.

"Somewhere at each location—if, based on the clues you're given, you correctly figure out where to go—a single magical container of some sort will appear to you, with seven identical objects inside," Muse Urania replied.

"Seven teams. So that's one clue for each," Persephone heard someone whisper.

"Just open the container and take out one of the objects," the teacher went on. "Collect one from each of the four locations before you return to MOA. These four objects will constitute your proof."

After a brief scan of the room, Muse Urania added, "Now I will unlock your scroll-gadgets and you'll all receive a clue to your first location. Good luck and have fun!" With that she unrolled her scroll-gadget, which was purple rather than white. When she gave its screen a poke, all the students' scroll-gadgets fell open at once, each unrolling to a size of about six inches square.

Persephone, Antheia, Theseus, and Pirithous

were all examining their blank gadget screens when Makhai finally joined their group. "Never fear, I'm here!" he announced with a smile that bordered on a smirk. (Or possibly a smirk that bordered on a smile. With him it was impossible to tell.)

As if to show it off, Makhai grabbed the front edges of the knee-length dark purple cloak he wore over his tunic and threw it wide with a flourish. It looked brand-new. Kydoimos was wearing an identical cloak, Persephone noticed now. The boys had likely bought them at the same time.

"Nice cloak, dude," Theseus commented.

Makhai ignored him, probably thinking mortals were beneath him or something. "Bet you were worried I wasn't coming!" he said, looking at Persephone and the other immortals on their team.

"Not sure that would have been any great loss,"

Persephone muttered. The words just slipped out before she could stop them. She smacked a hand over her own mouth, but it was too late.

Pirithous laughed loudly. "Good one, Persephone!" he said in an admiring tone. But she felt bad about what she'd said.

To her surprise, Makhai bowed his head. "Sorry," he said. "I overslept." And indeed he did have a bad case of bedhead, as if he hadn't had time to comb his hair. Noticing her staring, he tried to slick it down with his palms.

Persephone wanted to apologize for criticizing him, but before she could think of how best to do it, the teams' scrolls began to chime all over the classroom.

Bling! Bling!

The competition had well and truly begun!

6

The First Clue

EAGERLY, PERSEPHONE POKED A FINGERTIP AT the flashing green triangle that had appeared in the middle of her open scroll-gadget. Everyone else in the classroom was doing the same thing. Instantly, a gold-colored head-only statue of some old guy popped up where the green triangle had been. On the base of the statue head was a name: THEOPHRASTUS.

She huddled together with her Team Four teammates. "I know this name!" she exclaimed in a hushed tone that wouldn't be overheard by the other teams. "Theophrastus is a scientist. One of his big interests is botany. I've even read one of his books: *Enquiry into Plants.*"

"Cool," Pirithous piped up, again in an admiring tone.

A moment later, the statue's mouth began to move in a weird fashion, speaking to them. It was gadget animation! This was a nice improvement from the gadgets they'd used in the Temple Games.

"Without further ado, here's your first clue," announced the on-screen golden head of Theophrastus. "A most interesting sight, a black-bird that's white." After a brief pause it added, "As noted by Pausanias."

Huh? Didn't all blackbirds have to be black?

Persephone wondered. Otherwise, why would they be called *black*birds? The classroom filled with murmurs of surprise. "I've never heard of a white blackbird. Have you?" she asked her teammates. They all shook their heads.

Theseus frowned. "And who's Pausanias?" As soon as the words were out of his mouth, his scroll *bling*ed. "Hold on a sec. Something new just popped up!" he said excitedly. "Maybe it's another clue!"

Pirithous frowned. "There's nothing new on my gadget."

"Or mine," Makhai reported.

Persephone and Antheia looked at their gadgets and then at the boys and shook their heads. Only Theseus's scroll-gadget had *bling*ed. "Not on ours either. So what have you got?" Persephone asked him. There was no audio this time, so she and the rest of Team Four crowded around him, trying to look at the words that had popped up on his screen. Theseus read them out in a quiet voice. "Pausanias, a geographer, is the author of the ten-book series *Description of Greece*."

Just then they heard someone from another team shout, "I bet Mr. Eratosthenes can help us!" This caused a stampede as teams rushed out the classroom door.

Pirithous cocked his head at Persephone. "Who is Mr. Eratosthenes?" he asked. *Bling!* He looked down at his scroll. "Oh. I see. He's MOA's librarian."

"So maybe we should we go to the library too?" Antheia asked the others. "Pausanias must have written something about white blackbirds in one of his books. The library probably has all ten of them!"

Persephone stared at her, thinking, then shook her

head. "Even if we left now, we'd be the last team to reach the library. Last to have a turn to look through the books or talk to Mr. Eratosthenes. Besides, maybe there's a faster way to find out what we need to know."

"Ha!" said Makhai, sounding frustrated. "Stop wasting time! The library is our best bet. Let's get going before we wind up losers!"

Pirithous scowled at him. "Calm down and let her explain. She might just have a better plan of action."

Persephone sent him a grateful glance. "Muse Urania told us our scroll-gadgets were 'new and improved,'" she reminded her teammates. "Back during the Temple Games they could only display messages and clues. They couldn't speak information and we also couldn't, um, *interact* with them. But a minute ago when Theseus and Pirithous asked questions, their scrolls gave them the answers. So maybe to get more answers, all we need to do is—"

"Ask!" Pirithous blurted out before Persephone could finish. He smiled at her. "Brilliant!"

She smiled back at him. "Thanks."

"Let me try," Antheia squealed. She looked at her scroll-gadget. "Can you tell us where to find the white blackbirds?" she asked Theophrastus.

Bling!

The scientist's mouth moved jerkily. "Yes," said the animated head. Then it stopped speaking.

They all waited a few seconds for the statue head to go on, but it stayed silent. Antheia shook her scroll-gadget. "Maybe mine's broken?"

"We could try asking mine," Persephone offered just as Makhai snapped his fingers.

"Duh, Antheia," he said. "You didn't get the response you were after because your question only required a yes or no answer. Watch this." He looked down at the golden head in the middle of his open scroll-gadget. "*Where* can we find white blackbirds?" he asked it.

Bling! "On Mount Cyllene," the head of Theophrastus replied.

"That's south of here on the Peloponnese peninsula," Persephone said excitedly. "Let's go!"

They tried to stuff their still-open scroll-gadgets in their pockets, but they were too big to fit. "What do you suppose we need to do to get our scroll-gadgets to close?" Theseus asked.

Snap! As soon as the word "close" left his lips, his scroll-gadget rolled itself up.

"Close!" the other four team members said quickly. *Snap! Snap! Snap! Snap!*

Seconds later they all dashed out the door of

the Science-ology classroom. What a surprise that Makhai had been the one to figure out why Antheia's question hadn't resulted in the information they needed, Persephone thought as everyone headed toward the Academy's front doors. She'd never given Makhai any credit for brains, she realized. If he was smarter than she'd believed him to be, might she have misjudged him in other ways as well?

She decided that, since they'd been thrown together on the same team anyway, she would make an effort to get to know him a bit better. And act more kindly toward him. Starting now.

"Good job with the clue, Makhai," she called out to him as Team Four raced to the Academy's domed entrance. Although he didn't reply, a surprised, pleased expression flitted over his face and then was gone.

All five members of their team skidded to a stop by the communal basket of winged sandals that sat beside the heavy bronze doors that led outside. Following Persephone's lead, Antheia and Makhai shucked off their regular sandals and each grabbed a pair of winged ones.

Copying the MOA students, Theseus and Pirithous did the same. "Whoa," they chorused in surprise as the sandals' straps magically twined around their ankles.

As the silver wings at the heels of their sandals began to flutter, Persephone, Antheia, and Makhai rose to hover a few inches above the floor.

"Hey, mine aren't working," Pirithous said in a disappointed voice when the wings at his heels failed to flap.

Theseus frowned. "Neither are mine."

Makhai smiled at them smugly. "Sandals don't work for mortals."

"It's okay," Persephone told Pirithous and Theseus while adjusting the straps of her backpack to make them a bit tighter. "You'll each just need to hold hands with one of us immortals. Then your wings will fly too."

"Whoa! Fantastic!" Pirithous's eyes sparkled as he grabbed Persephone's hand. "You're stuck with me now," he teased, wobbling a bit as the wings at his heels finally began to work and he rose to hover beside her.

Persephone laughed. "No problem. Important tip: Don't let go or you'll fall."

Antheia grabbed Theseus's hand. "You can fly with me," she told him.

"Good," said Makhai, watching as Theseus also

rose to hover above the floor. "I'll fly faster without some mortal dragging me down."

Ignoring the sour boy (she certainly hadn't misjudged him on *that* trait!), Persephone smiled at Pirithous. "Ready?"

"Ready," he replied with a nod of his blond head.

The two of them pushed through the bronze doors. Then, with their teammates following, they zipped over the granite steps and sped across the courtyard before their sandals' wings took them into the bright blue sky.

7

Pirithous Problems

WOW!" EXCLAIMED PIRITHOUS AS HE AND Persephone circled the Academy before heading for Mount Cyllene. "I've never seen Mount Olympus Academy from the air before. It looks amazing!"

"Yeah. Doesn't it?" Persephone agreed, glancing down. Five stories high and built of polished white stone, the Academy was surrounded on all sides by dozens of Ionic columns—each one looked like a capital letter *I*, with a curlicue on each end of its top and bottom horizontal bars.

Sculpted below the Academy's peaked rooftop were finely chiseled low-relief friezes of various gods and goddesses engaged in scholarly feats. Everyone at MOA was proud to attend the school. Persephone felt sooo lucky that Zeus had invited her years ago, since not all immortals (and only very few mortals, like Heracles and Pandora) got to go here. Another thing to be grateful for!

Their journey took them almost directly south from Mount Olympus. As she and Pirithous flew, Persephone kept them beneath the cloud line for a better view of the towns, villages, farms, mountains, lakes, and rivers below.

"This is fantastic!" Pirithous enthused, turning his head this way and that to peer at everything they passed over. "If I could make these sandals work on my own, I'd fly all the time!"

His enthusiasm was infectious. Flying was nothing new to Persephone, so she'd begun to take her ability to zip through the skies for granted. Now she took the time to enjoy the sights and feel grateful for this too.

"Hey, look!" Pirithous shouted a short time later. "That's Larissa below—where I live. I recognize the theater. It's the biggest in the whole Thessaly region!"

Persephone glanced down. The large open-air theater below them was similar to most theaters in Greece. Built into the side of a hill, it was shaped like a huge bowl, with the stage at the bottom and terraced benches running up the sides.

"Wow! It's nice," she told him. As they sailed

beyond it, she asked, "So how did you and Theseus meet, anyway? And how long have you been friends?"

"We met four years ago, when we were eight years old, at a play at that very theater," Pirithous informed her. "During intermission a bunch of us decided to act out one of the play's battle scenes using wooden swords. This older boy thwacked Theseus hard on the arm. Theseus was super brave, though. He didn't cry out but just kept on fighting."

Pirithous paused and smiled, as if remembering that moment. Then he went on. "Later, when some girl hit my leg hard enough to make me fall, I jumped up and kept on fighting too. He and I were so impressed with each other's bravery that we switched seats to watch the rest of the play together so we could critique all the fight moves. We've been friends ever since."

"What a great story," said Persephone. "Speaking of friends . . ."

Looking around, she checked on the rest of their teammates. Antheia and Theseus had been flying a few hundred feet ahead of her and Pirithous for quite some time now. Glancing over her shoulder, she saw that Makhai was not far behind them. She scanned all directions. "I don't see any of the other teams," she said to Pirithous. "If we did choose the correct destination, it looks like we're off to a good head start."

"Yeah, fingers crossed," he said. "We keep this up and we're sure to win!"

"You think?" Persephone grinned. Already she was picturing the shelf by her bed in the dorm, where she could display her trophy once she had it. Or maybe she'd put it in her bedroom at home instead. *Hmm.*

As they continued to fly along, Pirithous began to pepper her with questions about her favorite activities (gardening and cheer team), food (a tie between nectaroni and cheese and yogurt with pomegranola), and color (possibly yellow, but she did like her new salmon-colored chiton a lot). He seemed to want to know everything there was to know about her!

But when she began to tell him about Hades, Pirithous abruptly changed the subject. "Theseus and I will have to leave MOA after dinner tonight," he told her. He smiled at her sadly. "I wish I could stay longer. Then we'd have time to get to know each other better."

Did he mean as friends? Something about his tone gave her the impression that he might be crushing on her. Was he? Persephone wondered. She couldn't very well ask him, because what if she was wrong?

That would be embarrassing. Even worse, though, what if she was right?

Aphrodite would probably be able to tell if Pirithous was crushing, but she wasn't here, unfortunately. Persephone bit her lip in confusion. Surely this mortal boy had read in *Teen Scrollazine* how she and Hades hung out together a lot. Though Pirithous's attention was flattering, her heart belonged to that godboy.

Thinking about Hades made Persephone wish she were flying with him right now. They wouldn't need to hold hands, since he was immortal, like her, but they probably would have anyway.

She and Pirithous were silent for a while, each thinking their own thoughts. If Hades saw her holding hands with him, would he be at all jealous? He never seemed to be. Not even that one time when the mega–pop star Orpheus had pulled her up onto the stage during a performance, autographed her arm, and even given her a kiss! (Just a quick, light one on the cheek.)

Thinking about that made her regret her jealous feelings toward Minthe yesterday even more. Next time she saw that girl, if ever, she'd be over-the-top nice to her to make up for her earlier jealousy, she decided. Maybe she'd even suggest some planting ideas to beautify her river or something.

By now she and her teammates were flying over the Gulf of Corinth, which separated mainland Greece from the Peloponnese peninsula. One of her back-pack straps had gotten tangled. As she untwisted it with her free hand, she noticed that way, way behind her and Pirithous, she could just make out the fig-ures of students from other teams. Either they, too, had learned that they could ask questions of the new and improved scroll-gadgets, or they'd found out the location of the white blackbirds at the library.

She was about to point out the approach of the others to the rest of her team when Pirithous's hand abruptly slipped from her grasp. Without her immortal magic to keep him aloft, he began to plummet straight down toward the waters of the gulf!

"Help!" he cried out. "Save me!"

Persephone's eyes widened in horror. Panicking, she swooped down and grabbed his hand again only seconds before he would have plunged into the gulf waters.

"Ye gods! I'm so, so sorry!" she apologized as she pulled him back upward to safety. She was always so careful when flying with mortals. How could this have happened?

Pirithous brushed his long blond hair out of his eyes and gave her a huge smile. "Thanks, Persy. I *knew* you'd rescue me!"

Huh? He didn't seem that upset, she thought suspiciously. Had he let go of her hand on purpose? Had this been some kind of a *test*? Or some oddball attempt to make her like him? Didn't he realize the danger he'd put himself in? And what was up with calling her *Persy*? She didn't really like nicknames. Before she could decide what to say to him, Makhai caught up to them.

Naturally, he'd seen what had happened. Zooming in circles around them, he taunted, "Good job, *Klutz*-ef-phoney. Not!"

Great, another nickname she didn't want. Argh!

Makhai's gaze moved to Pirithous, then back to her. "Can't say one mortal would be much loss, but still . . . Zeus would be mad if you'd actually doom-dropped this guy to smithereens." He grinned as if he'd just made the funniest joke ever.

Pirithous tightened his grip on Persephone's hand as his other hand clenched. With narrowed eyes, he shook his fist at Makhai. "You leave her alone!" he spat out. "She saved my life!"

Makhai's eyes widened. "Whoa, buddy. Take it easy. I was only messing with you. Can't you take a joke?"

"Sure," Pirithous replied. "But if that was your idea of a joke, you should probably stop trying to tell them."

"Huh?" Makhai frowned.

Uh-oh, thought Persephone. Mortals should know better than to insult an immortal. Especially one as bad-tempered as Makhai.

"You are not funny, dude," Pirithous went on, putting himself at even more risk for retaliation. He unballed his fist and flicked his fingers. "Why don't you show us how fast you can make your winged sandals fly and buzz off, god-dude!"

To Persephone's surprise, Makhai did exactly that. His dark purple cloak billowed behind him as he sped on ahead of her and Pirithous. She grinned at the blond mortal boy. He sure knew how to handle Makhai! He grinned back at her, looking a bit like a lovesick puppy.

Uh-oh. Before he could get the wrong idea and think she was flirting with him or something, she said sternly, "Hang on tight from now on. I can't have you falling again."

"Don't worry," he said, squeezing her fingers. "I won't let go." Then he blushed a deep cherry red.

For Zeus's sake! He *was* crushing on her. She was almost sure of it! Now she *really* wished Aphrodite were here. An expert at deflecting crushes without hurting feelings, she'd know how to handle this. But boys didn't crush on Persephone every day like they did on Aphrodite. They practically tripped over themselves to do that goddessgirl's bidding. Thinking all this, she began to sympathize with Hades' seeming inability to deal with Minthe's one-sided crush on him. It wasn't easy!

"C'mon. We'd better hurry," she told Pirithous briskly, "or the other teams will catch up to us." Hearing her, her winged sandals picked up their pace. In a blur of speed they dashed on toward Mount Cyllene.

8

The White Blackbird

THE MINUTE HER WINGED SANDALS TOUCHED down near the top of the snow-dusted mountain, Persephone dropped Pirithous's hand. "Look, there's the rest of our team," she told him, pointing. Their teammates, Antheia, Theseus, and Makhai, already stood some fifty feet ahead of them, staring up at a small stand of scrubby trees. At least a couple dozen blackbirds (*black* ones, not white ones) were roosting in the tops of the trees' branches. They flapped their wings and cawed up a storm as Persephone and Pirithous approached.

"Haven't seen any white ones like the gadget told us to find," Antheia called out as Persephone and Pirithous hurried to join their teammates.

"Oh. Too bad," said Persephone. "Maybe if we keep watching, one might come along in a few minutes?"

"Let's hope so. We need to hurry. The other teams aren't far behind us," said Theseus. He nodded toward Pirithous. "Let's walk farther down the mountain. Maybe the white blackbirds don't roost at this high altitude."

"I'll come too," said Makhai.

Persephone and Antheia shared a look. Apparently the company of mortal boys was preferable to the godboy over that of girls, even if the girls were immortal. They both laughed.

"Who needs 'em," Antheia joked as the three boys darted off.

Persephone giggled, then looked around. "Hey, you know what? I think this is where Hermes was born," she told Antheia. "In a cave somewhere on this mountain."

Hermes was a familiar sight at MOA. He ran a delivery service, and his mighty white-winged silver chariot was constantly crisscrossing Greece to deliver packages, and sometimes messages, to and from MOA and elsewhere. Occasionally he even gave rides to students. When Zeus had suddenly remembered he had a daughter living down on Earth and summoned her to Mount Olympus, for example, Hermes had picked Athena up and flown her to the Academy for her first day of school. (Zeus was amazing, but he could be quirky like that. Plus he had a thunderous temper sometimes if things didn't go his way!)

"Really?" said Antheia as they both wandered nearby, their eyes peeled for birds with white feathers. "I never knew that about Hermes. Too bad he's not here now, bringing us a message about where to find those white birds!"

"Hey! Over here. We see something!" Theseus shouted in their direction.

Immediately, the girls rushed off toward the three boys. When they caught up to them, Theseus held a finger to his lips and pointed up at a particular scrubby tree not far away. *Caw! Caw!* A group of blackbirds was roosting in that tree too.

"Look! Is that a white one?" Antheia pointed eagerly to the top of the tree.

Persephone gasped. It *was* a white bird. Almost the same size and shape as a blackbird, only white! As everyone began to exclaim over the white blackbird, however, she felt a seed of doubt take root and begin to grow inside her.

"The white bird is slightly smaller than the other blackbirds," she noted aloud. And now that she looked more closely, she saw that it had some brown on it. "And its head is more gray than white. In fact, it looks an awful lot like the snow finches I see in winter at the feeder in my backyard at home." A new thought popped into her head. "Hey, remember what Muse Urania told us back in class? 'Sometimes we see what we want or expect to see.' Think this could be an example of that?"

"Of us only *wanting* it to be a white blackbird, you mean?" asked Pirithous.

Persephone nodded.

"So you don't think it's a white blackbird, then?" Antheia asked, a look of disappointment on her face. "You think we need to keep looking?"

"No, I don't think it's a white blackbird," Persephone said in answer to Antheia's first question. "But I'm also guessing we don't need to keep looking."

Her teammates stared at her. "What? Why?" they murmured.

"Because I'm pretty sure we've found the bird Muse Urania intended us to find," Persephone told them. At their blank looks, she hurried to explain further. "When Muse Urania warned us that sometimes we see what we want or expect to see, I think she was hinting that that bird-watcher author guy Pausanias was mistaken in his identification. He wanted to discover an unusual bird so much that he tricked himself into believing it was a white blackbird."

Antheia nodded slowly. "I bet you're right. And I bet that after this contest one of Muse Urania's lectures will be about how naturalists sometimes make mistakes."

"Right," said Persephone. "For example, even though I'm the goddessgirl of spring and growing things, I've made plenty of mistakes identifying various plants. Once I even mistook a patch of the herb marjoram for oregano, for godness' sake."

When the others only looked at her blankly again, she went on. "They do look kind of alike, but it was a beginner's mistake." She chuckled. "Of course, I was only four years old at the time, so I guess I could cut myself some slack for that one."

"Enough talk," Makhai said impatiently. "If we've

found the bird Muse Urania wanted us to find, we'll soon know." With that he pulled his scroll-gadget from his pocket. The others did likewise. *Pzzt!* Suddenly a beam of green light shot downward from each of their tightly rolled scroll-gadgets.

As if attracted to one another by a powerful magnet, the beams joined together to make a circle of light on the ground. And within that circle of light, a carved wooden box appeared. It had fancy, swirly designs on it and was about the same size as a jewelry box. A moment later the beams fizzled away, but the box remained.

"Wait!" yelled Persephone, as Theseus dashed over and picked it up. "Don't open it. Pandora found a box like that one time. It was filled with trouble bubbles, and when they floated out, they caused all kinds of problems!"

"Yeah, I remember that," said Antheia. "Those bubbles made everybody act really weird. Aphrodite even pumped her hand under one armpit to make fart noises. Which was so *not* like her."

Pirithous and Theseus laughed, while Makhai snickered.

Still holding the box, Theseus ran one hand over his dreadlocks and glanced around their group. "Muse Urania told us we'd find a magical container at each geo-dashing location, right? This one's obviously magical, with the green beams and all. We have to open it and take one of the objects inside as proof of where we've been."

"Okay. Sorry," Persephone said, remembering. "I guess that means we really did solve the riddle. I wasn't sure. And after that Pandora incident, all wooden boxes make me a bit nervous."

While Theseus began fiddling with the box to try to open it, Makhai snorted. "That's dumb."

Heat rose in Persephone's cheeks. But she was determined to ignore his insult. "I guess we all have things that make us nervous," she said in as bright a voice as she could manage. "Even you, maybe?"

"Yeah, like sniffing your underarms to see if they're stinky?" Theseus said slyly. When Makhai gave him the stink-eye, he backed away grinning. "Hey, me and Pirithous saw you do it when you tripped over Persephone's scrolls yesterday in the hall. Just sayin'."

When Pirithous laughed, she flashed him and Theseus smiles. Immediately afterward, she regretted it, though. Because Pirithous's smile went megabright. Had she given him the idea that she felt the same way about him that he seemed to feel about her? As in a *crushing* way? They'd only met like an hour ago. Still, Aphrodite had told her once that love at first sight was a real thing. So maybe he felt that? Even if she didn't?

When Antheia and Makhai went over to help Theseus struggle with the box, Persephone suggested to Pirithous, "Hey, why don't you fly with Makhai for a while? Get to know each other."

Makhai stopped prying at the box to look over at them. "Uh, no, I don't think so," he said, shaking his head.

Luckily, Theseus managed to pop open the lid of the wooden box just then, shifting everyone's attention. Inside were seven identical bird-shaped figurines—one for each team, presumably—about three inches tall. They'd been chiseled from white stone.

"Could you put this in your backpack?" Theseus

asked, handing a bird figure to Persephone. "It seems you're the only person on our team who brought one."

"Sure," said Persephone. She slipped off her backpack, opened it, and stowed the stone figurine inside.

Before Theseus could set the box back down on the ground, Pirithous stopped him. "Wait! Can I have a look at the figures? I'm wondering if they're all exactly the same. I mean, what if one is better than the other in terms of winning the game, you know?"

Theseus passed the box to him, and Pirithous examined the small stone birds, picking up one after another. "Nah, I guess they look identical," he murmured slowly.

"Hey, lemme see those," said Makhai just as

shouts sounded from overhead. Everyone looked up as members of Team One—Athena, Iris, Heracles, Ares, and Kydoimos—began to set down around them in their winged sandals. Athena was holding hands with Heracles, since he was a mortal and couldn't fly on his own. (Since they were each other's crushes, Persephone was sure neither of them minded!)

"Rats. We shouldn't have stood out here in the open like this where they could spot us. We gave away the location of the first clue," said Pirithous, sounding frustrated.

"Maybe. Or maybe they were coming here already anyway," said Theseus. "That Athena's called a 'brain' for a reason, you know? You wouldn't believe how many things Heracles told me she invented— ships, the chariot, the plow, weaving, the flute, the trumpet, and more. She even invented the olive. Team One is going to be our biggest competition."

"Yeah, no joke," said Pirithous. He pounded a fist into the palm of his other hand. "I want a trophy! Mistakes like this aren't helping."

Persephone wanted a trophy too, but not as much as Pirithous, apparently. He seemed *really* mad and a little desperate. And his expression became even more annoyed by what happened next. The white blackbird (or snow finch?) was still perched on the straggly tree beyond them, and Athena and the rest of Team One caught sight of it right away.

"There it is!" Kydoimos yelled. As his teammates began exclaiming over it, a movement caught Persephone's attention. From the corner of her eye, she glimpsed Makhai stuffing the rest of the stone bird figures into his pockets. She blinked.

Huh? Had she seen what she thought she'd seen?

Just then Kydoimos glanced Makhai's way too. "Is that box the container we were supposed to find?" he asked.

Makhai quirked an eyebrow in his direction. "Maybe," he said unhelpfully.

"C'mon, quit wasting our time," Ares groused. He'd landed next to Kydoimos, and now he stepped over to Makhai and held out his hands for the box. Makhai's eyes went a little shifty. Still holding on to it, he began to back away.

Impatiently, Ares tapped the toe of one of his sandals. "Hand it over!" he commanded. As the godboy of war, he could be pretty intimidating, so finally Makhai held out the box to him. But as soon as Ares touched it, it disappeared!

"I think your team will need to cross the beams

of your scroll-gadgets to make it reappear," Antheia said. Just then, all of Team Four's scroll-gadgets went *bling!*

"Don't help them!" yelled Makhai as Team One quickly did what Antheia had suggested. Ignoring the new message on her scroll-gadget for now, Persephone watched the box reappear on the ground within the circle of green light that Athena's team's gadgets had created.

In an instant, the beams disappeared. Athena picked up the box. The lid lifted easily this time. Makhai seemed to freeze when she popped it open to reveal the remaining six carved bird figures. Persephone saw him ram a hand deep into one of his pockets, then quietly gasp in surprise and yank his hand back out.

What was up with that? she wondered.

"Oh, how adorable," said Iris, peering at the figures inside the box. Athena took out one of the white stone birds and gave it to Heracles to hold in a leather drawstring bag that was tied to his belt. Then she looked down into the box again. "Five left, I see. I guess that means we're the first two teams to arrive here and solve the first clue?"

"Uh-huh," Antheia replied. As Athena closed the lid of the box and set it back down on the ground, it magically disappeared again.

Persephone's mind was racing. If there were five figurines left in the box after two had been removed, Makhai couldn't have taken more. She'd been so certain she'd seen him stuffing them into his pockets. If he hadn't done that, then why had he seemed so nervous, and why had he checked his pockets? It was all very odd. But clearly he hadn't cheated the other teams out of getting their proof after all. Which was a good thing.

Maybe this was another example of "seeing what she expected to see," she mused. In the past, Makhai and Kydoimos *had* been known to cheat. Once they'd even stolen an answer key from Muse Urania's desk for a Science-ology quiz. So maybe she'd expected the worst of him.

Bling! Persephone's thoughts were interrupted by the sound of a new message arriving on Team One's scroll-gadgets. Undoubtedly it was a repeat of the same message that Team Four had gotten just moments ago. After that message had arrived, she'd glimpsed Pirithous talking to his scroll-gadget and tapping away on it feverishly even as she'd been watching Athena and Makhai. So at least he'd read the message and gotten the next clue. Her team had better move fast, because now Team One had caught up to them!

As Team One moved away to huddle together with their scroll-gadgets, Persephone unrolled hers at last and tapped on the flashing green triangle. The golden head of Theophrastus appeared. "We love frolicking in waves and sunning ourselves on beaches," it said. "To see us is an omen of good fortune. Our image is even on a coin! Can you find us?"

9

Clue Two

PERSEPHONE AND HER TEAMMATES QUICKLY formed their own huddle some distance away from Team One, so that they could discuss the new message clue in secret. "Got to be some kind of sea creature," she said.

"Yeah, this must be the clue Poseidon made up, since it's about the sea," Makhai said in a low voice.

"I'm going to check all my coins," Theseus

said, emptying his pockets of drachmas and obols. "Anybody else got money?" He spoke quietly and turned away from Athena's team so they wouldn't see what he was doing and think of doing the same thing.

No one else on Persephone's team had coins, unfortunately.

Pirithous drifted away from the group again to continue tap-tap-tapping on his scroll-gadget. What could he possibly be doing? Persephone wondered. But her attention was drawn away from him when Antheia whispered, "Maybe the sea creature is a dolphin. They like to frolic in waves."

"True," said Persephone. "But I've never seen them lying around on sunny beaches."

She bent over her scroll-gadget. "How long can dolphins survive on land?" she asked the head of Theophrastus.

In its jerky fashion, the golden head replied: "Most dolphins can only survive for a few hours on land before becoming dehydrated, especially in warm weather. Because they don't have the proper limbs to walk on land, they can become stuck in sand and unable to return to the sea."

"So, not likely to be a dolphin," Antheia said disappointedly.

"Aha!" Theseus crowed suddenly. He did a little happy dance. Then, remembering that Team One was nearby, he huddled with his Team Four teammates (all except Pirithous, who was still tapping on his scroll-gadget a short distance away) and held up a coin. "Monk seal," he said, passing it around so they could see the image of its head on the coin.

"How long can seals survive on land?" Persephone asked her scroll-gadget.

"Who cares?" scoffed Makhai. "We just need to find some so we can get our next proof!"

Antheia scowled at him.

Persephone glanced at Theseus. "I don't doubt that you're right about us needing to search for monk seals. I'm only curious to know the answer."

Bling! This time she got a written reply.

"What's it say?" Pirithous asked, coming over to rejoin the group. He took a look at Theseus's coin, then handed it back to him. For some reason, there was a self-satisfied smile on Pirithous's face, as if he'd been the one to figure out the message clue instead of Theseus.

Persephone read the reply aloud: "'Most seals are able to spend several days to a week out of the water. If you see one on the beach, it's usually because it wants to be there and isn't in trouble or anything.'"

"Here's an even better question: Where's the best place to *find* monk seals?" Pirithous asked his scroll-gadget. *Bling!* "'Monk seals are numerous in parts of the Mediterranean, especially the Aegean Sea,'" he read aloud.

Antheia pointed upward just then. "Uh-oh." Persephone looked skyward to see that Team One was leaving.

"They must be figuring things out ahead of us," said Theseus, "Let's get a move on!" As he said this, three more of the seven Science-ology teams touched down on the mountainside to look for the white blackbird.

For some reason, Pirithous just calmly grinned at the departing and arriving teams. "Don't worry. I have a feeling we've got this competition in the bag," he said, wearing a sneaky expression.

Persephone wished she felt as confident as he sounded. Already she was untying the laces that bound the wings at her sandals' heels. Recalling her concern about the mortal boy's seeming crush on her, she was about to suggest again that he fly with Makhai for a while, when Makhai launched upward ahead of the rest of them. His purple cloak billowed around him in the wind as he flew off. Maybe she could get Theseus to trade? Too late! Pirithous grabbed her hand before she could suggest that.

"Woo-hoo!" Pirithous yelled. As they rose into the air again, he seemed in strangely high spirits. He did funny poses to make her laugh, like moving his hands and kicking his feet as if he were swimming up through water. "Flying is awesome!" he shouted to the skies. When Persephone giggled at his enthusiasm (it was impossible not to be affected by it), he gave her a sweetly goofy puppy-dog look. "Especially with you, Persy."

Argh!

After flying back over the Gulf of Corinth again, Persephone and her teammates headed overland in a northeast direction. "I don't see Team One," Theseus called out. "Think they were misled by the clue?"

Persephone shook her head and called back, "Doubt it. Like you said, Athena's really smart. If we could figure out the right answer, I'm sure her team did too."

"Doesn't seem like Team One could have gotten *that* far ahead of us already," Makhai shouted over.

Persephone nodded and glanced around. "Yeah. Maybe they're looking for monk seals in some other body of water? I hope we haven't made a mistake in *our* thinking."

"Don't worry," Pirithous told her as they flew north of the city of Athens, named after the super-smart Athena. "Like I said, I just know we're going to win this competition. And trophies, too! I've never won one before."

"Me either," said Persephone, feeling momentarily encouraged by his certainty. "I mean, I'd like that too. But how can you be so sure of a win?"

"Oh, just a hunch," he said matter-of-factly, but his eyes looked a bit shifty, like Makhai's often did. "Athena may be smart, but so am I. And, unlike her, I'll do almost anything to get what I want."

Leaping Olympians! thought Persephone. This boy had more confidence than any mortal she'd ever met! Except maybe Heracles. Or did Pirithous know something the rest of them didn't?

They'd reached the near shore of the Aegean Sea

when Makhai, who had slowed some to allow the others to catch up, gave a whoop. "Found some! Look!"

Sure enough, she saw a group of monk seals sunning themselves on the beach down below. The adults among them were mostly dark brown or black with light gray bellies, but the pups had black wooly coats with white or yellow patches on their bellies.

Wup! As her team swooped lower in their winged sandals, the playful growling sounds the seals were making became louder. *Wup! Wup! Wup!*

Persephone watched a young pup burrow its nose in the sand, then use one of its flippers to toss sand over its back. "Oh, how cute. They remind me of Cerberus a little bit."

When Pirithous raised an eyebrow at her in question, she added, "That's Hades' dog. He likes to lie around and relax too."

Overhearing, Antheia said, "I wonder what Hades and Muse Urania decided we'll have to search for in the Underworld—when we get to that clue."

Before anyone could hazard a guess, Makhai whipped out his scroll-gadget and shouted, "Scroll-gadgets at the ready, everyone!"

Still in the air, the rest of the team pulled their gadgets out too. Instantly, green beams shot from the tips of their scrolls again. The beams intersected at a point on the beach a safe distance from the seals they'd discovered.

And right at that spot another container appeared—this time a large pink clamshell. Yes, this was definitely Poseidon's clue, Persephone decided. Seals and shells and the sea all went together. She wondered if he and Hades had fashioned the containers and the objects that went with them as well as creating the clues. Probably. That would explain why they'd both been too busy to make it to the cafeteria for dinner last night, because just coming up with a clue didn't seem like it would've taken that much time.

All five team members zipped over to the shell in their winged sandals and landed. Either they'd been lucky enough to find the exact group of monk seals the clue was pointing toward, or *any* group of monk seals would've made the magic container appear, Persephone thought. Didn't matter. Either way, they'd been successful. What a relief!

Makhai got to the shell first and opened it. Inside were carved figurines of monk seals. They were about the same size as the bird figures had been, and shaped from some kind of hard black wood.

Persephone quickly counted the figures inside. "Seven!" she shouted in triumph. "Which must mean we're the first team this container has appeared to so far."

"Yes!" said Pirithous doing a happy fist pump.

With the rest of Team Four looking on, Makhai took out one of the black wood figures. He handed it to Persephone so she could slip it into her backpack to join the bird. "Too bad we can't take all of them," he remarked. "Then, even if another team got ahead of us, they wouldn't have proof they were here."

"No way. That would be cheating!" Antheia protested.

"So? I'm in this to win this!" said Makhai. "But you can relax anyway. Those figures are steal-proof. They've got some kind of magic spell on them to prevent any team from taking more than one."

Persephone frowned at him. "And you know that because . . . ?"

Makhai avoided her eyes. "I figured it out. That's all."

Humph, thought Persephone. It seemed she'd been right about him trying to pocket all the bird figures back at Mount Cyllene. Luckily, the container's magic had somehow stopped him!

"I'd rather lose than not play fair and square," she informed him. And this was true. Much as she longed to have a trophy, how could she enjoy it if she knew their team had only won because they'd cheated?

"I agree," said Theseus. He looked over at Makhai. "What you tried to do wasn't cool, dude."

Makhai had the decency to hang his head at this, even though the scolding was delivered by a mere mortal.

Pirithous shrugged. "I want to win this thing too,"

he said. "But Makhai's right. Taking all the figures won't work."

Huh? Had he also "just figured it out"? Persephone wondered. Were he and Makhai *both* would-be cheaters? She hoped not.

Suddenly Pirithous snatched a figure from the clamshell, which Makhai still held. "Here's how the magic works." He opened his hand wide so that the little wooden monk seal was easily visible on the palm of his hand. His teammates (all except Makhai, that was) gasped in surprise when the little wooden monk seal vanished from his hand seconds later. "Look," he said, tilting the open shell so everyone could peer inside.

Antheia leaned over to count the figures. "One, two, three, four, five, *six!*" she exclaimed. "The one you tried to take wound up back in the shell!"

Pirithous nodded. "I accidentally discovered the magic spell myself when I was examining the bird figures back in the first challenge to see if they were all identical. Which they were, by the way. But every time I picked up a figure, it would disappear from my fingers a few seconds later and reappear in the box. The container somehow senses when a team removes more than one figurine, and magically summons it back."

Phew, thought Persephone. Her concern a moment ago was wrong. It seemed that Pirithous had only been experimenting with the first container they'd found. He hadn't really been trying to steal its figures after all. But Makhai had!

"Anyway," Pirithous went on, as Makhai snapped shut the lid of the shell and set it on the beach, where it instantly vanished. "There are other ways to increase our chances of winning that don't involve stealing."

Bling! Before Persephone or anyone else could ask what he meant by this, their third clue message arrived.

"Yay, us!" Antheia said excitedly. "Only two locations to go!" She glanced over at Makhai. "We can win this fair and square, so no more attempts to cheat. Okay?"

Was it just her imagination, or did Makhai's face turn a shade pinker at this? Persephone wondered. Maybe his conscience was pricking him? Looking down at his sandals, he mumbled, "Okay."

"Time for our next clue!" Pirithous called out cheerily, drawing everyone's attention from Makhai. With that the teammates unrolled their scroll-gadgets and tapped on the green triangles to call up the statue head of Theophrastus.

Just then, shouts came from high overhead. They all glanced up. Persephone could see Teams Two and Six racing each other. Some of them glanced down and waved. They couldn't miss seeing the seals on the beach. Strangely, however, they didn't stop, but only continued to sail over the gulf and then head south. "Where in the world could they be going?" she wondered aloud.

Pirithous chuckled. "Seems like they're a bit confused about clue number two. Good luck to them, though!"

10

The Last Two Clues

THE THIRD CLUE WAS AN EASY ONE: *WE GROW ON low shrubs in sunny meadows with dry, rocky soil. Our delicate petals never last long, but every day we bloom afresh.*

Easy for Persephone and Antheia, at least, given their knowledge of botany. Neither had any trouble identifying the described shrub as a rock rose. After they high-fived over their mutual guess, their team began winging its way in a northeasterly direction over the Aegean toward Asia Minor. Turned out the girls just happened to know of a large meadow of rock roses that grew on the island of Cisthene, across from the island of Lesbos.

The shrubs in the sunny meadow were in full bloom, covered with pink and yellow flowers, each with five petals that looked and felt like papyrus. "Mmm. Don't you love their scent?" Persephone said to Pirithous after inhaling deeply. To her nose, the leaves of the rock roses smelled like a mix of honey and pine.

"Mm-hmm," Pirithous replied distractedly. He was fiddling with his scroll-gadget again, doing who knew what. He'd barely even glanced at the roses after Persephone had carefully landed with him in a grassy spot between shrubs so as not to crush any of the delicate blossoms.

145

Makhai pulled his scroll-gadget from his pocket. "Come on, everyone. No time to lose. Let's cross beams so we can get the next proof object and get out of here."

"In a few minutes," said Pirithous, continuing to tap away. "Besides, there's no real hurry," he added in a casual tone. "We're way ahead of the other teams."

Knowing how much Pirithous wanted to win— as much as or more than the rest of their team— Persephone was surprised to hear him say this, even if it probably was true. She took her scroll-gadget from her pocket to be at the ready.

Suddenly Antheia, who'd also been sniffing the roses, gave a little cry. "Oh no! My scroll-gadget isn't in my pocket. It must have dropped out!" She began searching for it among the roses nearby.

"I'll help," Persephone said. After re-pocketing

her gadget, she got down on her hands and knees to search among the rosebushes. Theseus did the same. Makhai let out a huge sigh of frustration and annoyance, but then he began to help too. Pirithous, however, didn't even look up from his scroll-gadget.

Persephone had only been searching for a minute or two when her stomach growled, reminding her she'd had nothing to eat since breakfast. Sitting back on her heels, she shrugged off her backpack and pulled a pomegranola bar from a compartment at the front of it. She'd stuffed five bars inside, along with five apples. "Anyone hungry besides me?" she called out to the rest of her team. Since no one else had thought to bring a bag or pack, she was pretty sure nobody else had snacks with them. Luckily, being *dependable*, she'd brought extra. Enough for her whole team, in fact.

"I am!" Antheia called out from the patch of ground she was searching just a few feet from Persephone.

"Me too," said Theseus, who was maybe ten feet beyond the girls.

Persephone tossed a pomegranola bar to each of them. Then she glanced over at Makhai, who was thrashing around in some bushes to her left. She held up the next-to-last pomegranola bar. "How about you, Makhai? Want one?"

"Me? Really?" he said, coming to a standstill. He seemed surprised that she'd offered him one. Maybe bullies (and would-be cheaters) didn't expect kindnesses, since they never offered them. Her heart softened toward him a little and she tossed him the bar.

"Thanks," he said as he caught it. He even gave her a crooked smile.

Antheia leaned toward her and murmured, "Makhai being nice and polite? I think I'm going to faint."

Persephone grinned. Maybe deep, deep, *deep* down that godboy wasn't so bad.

But then Makhai squinted at the girls as if he suspected they were making fun of him. He looked at the bar Persephone had shared and then back at her. "Is there something wrong with this pomegranola bar? Is it bespelled to make my hair fall out or something?" He sniffed it suspiciously.

Persephone sighed. "There's nothing wrong with it, I promise. It's just an ordinary pomegranola bar. I'll trade mine with you, see?" She went over and gave him her bar in exchange for his. Then, because she was curious, she added softly, "Do you always expect a trick when someone is nice to you?"

Makhai appeared to think about this for a moment. "Yeah," he said at last. "Better suspicious and safe than sorry and hairless." His words made her feel even softer toward him. How sad to constantly worry that others' kindnesses weren't genuine!

Persephone had planned to ask Pirithous if he wanted the last snack bar, but to tell the truth she was a little peeved that he was still fiddling with his scroll-gadget while everyone else on their team was trying to help Antheia find hers. If he was hungry, he could ask for it, she decided.

A glance up at the sky told her that it must be around noon, since the sun was directly overhead. By midafternoon the petals of the rock roses in the meadow would drop off, but fresh new flowers would appear on the shrubs by tomorrow morning.

When ten more minutes of searching didn't turn up the missing scroll-gadget, Antheia said sadly, "I never checked that I still had my gadget after we left the monk seals to fly here. It could have fallen out anywhere. It might even be at the bottom of the Aegean!"

"You should have been more careful with it," groused Makhai.

"I know," moaned Antheia.

"Could have happened to any of us," Theseus said kindly. Before Persephone could voice her agreement, he added, "It's possible we don't need all five of our beams to make a container appear. Shall we try with four?"

Makhai's eyes brightened at this. "Great idea, mortal!"

Theseus grinned at him. "We do have them once in a while," he said wryly. "Stop messing around and come join us," he called to Pirithous as the others gathered together to see if they could still bring forth a container with one less gadget.

"Oops. Sorry!" Pirithous closed his gadget. Then he jumped to his feet and went to join the rest of the team.

Luckily, four beams *were* enough to bring forth a container. But the clay-fired urn that appeared at the place where the beams intersected seemed kind of wavery. And it was having trouble settling on its shape. It grew taller and thinner, then shorter and fatter.

Worried that the urn could disappear before they got their proof object, Persephone pounced on the clay pot. The beautiful yellow glass roses inside seemed stable. Quickly, she plucked one of the seven roses from the ever-changing urn. She held it up so the others could see it, then tucked it safely away in her backpack. Afterward, she popped the lid back on the wavery urn. It disappeared the instant she plunked it down on the ground.

Bling!

"Woo-hoo!" shouted Antheia. "Only one more clue to go!" She must have been greatly relieved that they'd been able to summon the container without her scroll-gadget, thought Persephone. If she'd been in Antheia's place, she would've felt the same. Woo-hoo, indeed. Trophies were looking more and more likely for her and her team!

Now everyone unrolled their scroll-gadgets and tapped on the green triangles that appeared on their screens. Everyone except Antheia, of course. Smiling at her, Persephone stepped closer to her. "We can share mine." Since Muse Urania had said they'd be visiting four geo-locations in all, the next one would be their fourth and last clue.

"Thanks," said Antheia.

As they all knew it would, their last clue pointed to a location within the Underworld. "A lifeless stream with a voice of mourning, wild and dark and sulfurous," the golden head of Theophrastus recited.

Persephone's heart tightened inside her chest. "It's probably the River Cocytus in the Underworld," she informed her teammates. "The nymph caretaker of it is named Minthe. I met her yesterday."

Of all the places Hades could have chosen, why had he decided to send teams to that dismal, smelly location? she wondered. He could have sent them to the Elysian Fields! That was the Underworld's most desirable neighborhood, where only the luckiest of the dead got to go to feast, play, and sing forevermore. It was pretty much the opposite of the extremely icky Tartarus! And of the stinky Cocytus, too.

Bling! Suddenly, in bright red capital letters, the word CAUTION flashed onto their scroll-gadgets. Then Theophrastus appeared and spoke again. "For safety reasons, mortal teammates may not enter the Underworld. All mortals must wait for their respective teams outside the fenced entrance."

Persephone would bet a hundred—no, a *thousand* drachmas that Hades had insisted on that warning. The Underworld was way too dangerous for mortals.

"Aw, man. That is sooo unfair!" exclaimed Pirithous. From the frown on Theseus's face, Persephone could tell that he wasn't happy either about not being able to accompany their team to the river.

"Yeah, that really cuts down on the number of us able to work together to figure stuff out once we're there," noted Antheia.

Persephone shrugged. "Honestly, it's for your own good," she said to Pirithous and Theseus as she glanced from one to the other. "If you guys entered the Underworld, you could wind up stuck there forever!"

Before she could explain further, Pirithous spoke up again. "But Hades is in charge of the Underworld, right? Couldn't he bend the rules a little? Enough to make it safe for us to—"

"Nuh-uh," Persephone interrupted, shaking her head. "Hades may be in charge of the Underworld, but it's patrolled by Alecto, Megaera, and Tisiphone, these three wild-haired, snake-belted women—"

"I've heard of them. They're called the Furies," interrupted Makhai. He eyed Theseus and Pirithous while flicking pomegranola crumbs from his purple cloak. (Apparently he'd decided Persephone hadn't been trying to poison him after all, since he'd eaten the whole bar.) "You do *not* want to cross them," Makhai went on. "They're not likely to cut rule-breakers any slack."

"Yeah," said Antheia. "You know the rock star Orpheus? Well, his girlfriend and fellow band member, Eurydice, almost got stuck in the Underworld when she dared to go in. The Furies planned to keep her there forever!"

"And if Orpheus hadn't agreed to play for them and I hadn't named a flower after the foolish girl, they would have, too," Persephone added with a shudder.

"Named a flower after her?" Theseus repeated in confusion.

"Never mind," said Persephone. "It's a long story."

Pirithous shrugged. Appearing to finally accept that he and Theseus wouldn't be able to enter the Underworld once they arrived, he said, "I guess it's okay if Theseus and I have to wait this one out. We're way ahead of the other teams anyway. How many times do I have to say it? We. Are. Going. To. Win!" He pumped a confident fist in the air.

"Hope you're right. But until we win, we haven't won," said Theseus, sounding worried in spite of their lead.

Seconds later, Team Four took to the air again. "Follow me," Persephone told the others, as she headed for the Underworld.

"Happily," said Pirithous, who was once again holding her hand.

"Ha! You don't have a choice about following me, since you're flying with me," Persephone told him.

"Happily," he repeated.

Argh. Persephone rolled her eyes, which only made him smile . . . happily.

"I'm hungry," he informed her. "Got any more of those snack bars you were handing out earlier?"

"One more," she told him. "And there are also apples in my backpack."

"I'll get them," said Pirithous. Still holding on to her hand, he managed to twist and reach around so he could fish the snack bar and two red apples out of her backpack. He pocketed one of the apples for himself, handed her the other apple, and began eating the last pomegranola bar. They fell silent as they continued toward the Styx, both munching away. Pirithous devoured the snack bar in a few bites and then started in on his apple.

"It's kind of strange that we seem to be so far

ahead of all the other teams, don't you think?" Persephone remarked after they'd finished their apples and dropped the cores onto the earth below. It pleased her to think of the seeds possibly becoming trees where they landed.

A sneaky smile flashed across Pirithous's face. "Maybe. Maybe not."

Huh? His unexpected reply threw her off balance. *Literally.* As she shot him a look, they dipped sideways, and she almost lost hold of his hand.

"Whoa!" Pirithous cried out. But once she'd steadied them both, he grinned. "If you're not more careful, you might have to rescue me again!"

Don't count on it, she almost said. Truth was, Pirithous was getting on her nerves more and more, while at the same time Makhai was getting on her nerves less and less. How odd was that?

But then Muse Urania's words ran through her mind again. *Sometimes we see what we want or expect to see.* Had Persephone been *expecting to see* Makhai as totally awful all along? And to see Pirithous as . . . as what, exactly? Maybe not all good, but at least less *secretive*. Besides that, his insta-crush on her was getting mega-annoying. He'd only known her for a few hours, after all. No matter what Aphrodite believed about love at first sight, how real could such a fast crush be?

When they reached the River Styx at last, Persephone set down on the side of the river opposite the Underworld, near an iron fence Hades had built not long ago. The fence was meant to keep curious mortals from trying to sneak across the River Styx and enter the Underworld. To make his intentions to would-be trespassers super clear, he'd posted a huge sign on the fence that read NO MORTALS ALLOWED! And there were additional signs along the bank that said things like IF YOU'RE NOT A SHADE—SHOO! and KEEP OUT, UNLESS YOU'RE DEAD!

"Yikes! Hades isn't exactly friendly, is he?" said Pirithous, pointing to the signs.

"He's friendly," Persephone assured him, hearing the annoyance in her own voice at his comment. "Those warnings are for your own good, trust me."

Antheia touched down on the riverbank with Theseus not long after Persephone and Pirithous landed. And Makhai was right behind them. "Here. Take this," Theseus said, handing Antheia his scroll-gadget. "Since Pirithous and I will just be waiting here for the rest of you, I won't need it."

Antheia beamed at him. "Good idea. Thanks, Theseus."

"And maybe I should take yours," Persephone said to Pirithous. "We know that we can get a container to appear with only four beams. But as unsteady as that container was, three might be too few."

"Yeah, okay," said Pirithous. But he seemed a little reluctant as he handed it over.

"We shouldn't be gone long," Persephone assured both mortal boys. "Like I said, I know where the River Cocytus is. I was just there yesterday morning." With that she took off with the other two immortals on her team, holding a scroll-gadget in each of her hands.

Persephone was pleased to see that Minthe wasn't in sight when they arrived at her river. Fingers crossed she wouldn't have to deal with the gloomy girl at all. After she, Antheia, and Makhai strapped their sandals' wings so they'd stop flapping, the three of them walked up to the riverbank.

"Ew. Stink-eee," said Makhai, pinching his nose closed.

"Yeah, the sulfur smell is strong today," said Persephone, doing the same. Because . . . ick.

"No kidding," Antheia agreed. Holding her nose too, she stared down at the ugly, muddy river. "I've never been to the Underworld before," she said in a nasal voice. "Is the rest of it as awful as this place?"

"Thankfully not," answered Persephone as the three of them pointed all four scroll-gadgets toward the ground. Not wanting to leave Antheia and Makhai with a bad impression of Hades' realm, she added, "Actually, there are fields of these really pretty flowers called asphodel in some areas, and—"

But before she could continue, four beams of green light suddenly shot from the scroll-gadgets. The beams intersected at a spot only a few feet away on the riverbank. And right at that spot, a dog-shaped box appeared. Like the urn, it wavered and changed shape, so sometimes the dog had three heads, sometimes two, and sometimes just one.

As Makhai stepped forward to get the box, Persephone shrugged off her backpack so she could put the last object inside with the others. Watching her, Antheia handed her Theseus's scroll-gadget. "Could you please put this in your backpack for safekeeping? I'd hate to accidentally lose another one."

"Sure thing," said Persephone. To free her hands, she decided to slip all *three* scroll-gadgets—her own, Pirithous's, and Theseus's—into her pack.

Makhai had picked up the box by now. As he was about to open it, he suddenly hesitated. "Maybe you'd like to open this one?" he said, gallantly handing the box to Antheia.

Seeing this, Persephone couldn't help wondering if he might be paying forward her earlier kindness to him with the pomegranola bar. It would certainly be nice to think so!

With a look of surprise, Antheia accepted the wavery dog-shaped box. "Thanks," she said. Inside the golden-hinged box were seven bars of shiny gold, each and shaped like a dog-bone biscuit. "Wow!" she said as she lifted out one of the golden dog biscuits.

"Cool!" said Makhai.

Hot! thought Persephone, but she didn't say it out loud because she liked having the word be a private joke between her and Hades.

Antheia closed the lid of the box, but she hadn't yet set it down on the ground when the sulfur smell got to Persephone and made her cough. *Hack!* "I wish Hades had picked somewhere nicer—*hack!*—to send us so you'd get a better—*hack!*—impression of the Underworld. It's really not this—*hack!*—bad everywhere." He was so used to the smells here, he probably didn't realize how offensive they could be to visitors.

Perched in a gnarled tree on the opposite bank of the Cocytus, a screech owl let out a whiny, mournful cry. Makhai shivered. "Let's get out of here. This stinko river gives me the creeps." He untied the wings at his sandals' heels. Without waiting to see if the girls were doing the same, he took off back the way they had come, his purple cloak flapping behind him.

"I like how he waited for us. Such a gentleman . . . not," murmured Antheia while still holding the box. Then she corrected herself. "Although he *did* let me open the box. Boys can be hard to figure out."

"That's for sure," Persephone agreed. Sharing a look, both girls grinned.

"Makhai's right, though," Antheia noted. "This river *is* creepy. And so is the area around it."

"Mm-hmm. Could you imagine having to live here? Ugh," Persephone said, thinking of Minthe.

Antheia was bending to place the box on the ground when suddenly that very nymph rose from the yucky water just a few feet from where they stood on the bank. Minthe shook a finger at them, her beautiful face red with anger. "How dare you? When you insult my river, you insult me!"

Antheia straightened, then froze in alarm, her mouth gaping open. "Whoa! Who's that?" she whispered, nudging Persephone with an elbow.

"Minthe, the naiad who's the caretaker of this river," Persephone whispered back. "I mentioned her earlier, remember?"

Turning toward Minthe, she said in as polite

a tone as she could manage, "Hi, there. I'm Persephone. Remember me from yesterday? This is my friend Antheia from MOA." She waved a hand in the direction of the dog-shaped box. "We're doing a school project right now and had to get something from that box. But we're really sorry. We didn't mean to be unkind. Honestly. We were only—"

"Being rude, that's what you were doing!" Minthe interrupted. She took a step closer to the riverbank, causing the ooky brown water to swirl around her ankles. "Do you stuck-up goddessgirls think I like this stinky-dink smell? No way! I'd give anything not to be stuck here!"

She glared at Persephone, her eyes boring into her. "You're so lucky Hades likes you. I don't get why he does, though. You're nowhere near as beautiful as I am," she said with a sneer. Then, with a graceful motion, she reached with her free hand to fluff her gorgeous, long, moss-green hair.

Though the nymph's insults were hurtful, Persephone recognized the frustration and envy beneath her words, in much the same way she'd begun to glimpse the fear of unkind treatment that underlay Makhai's bad behavior. Before Persephone could say something to try to calm Minthe, however, Antheia found her tongue.

"Hades is the lucky one!" she told the nymph. She narrowed her eyes. "Ever heard the saying that beauty is only skin deep? Well, from what I've seen of you so far, you're a good example of that, Minthe. Because you don't seem like a very nice person inside. Persephone is cooler and nicer than practically anyone else I know! Pretty, too. And why don't you clean this place up if you don't like it?" Still clasping the box, she flung one arm wide to indicate the river and its banks. "Maybe you're just too lazy?"

Uh-oh, thought Persephone. While it was sweet of her friend to leap to her defense, she could tell from the look in Minthe's eyes that Antheia had only succeeded in making her angrier. Did part of that anger spring from embarrassment? On some level, Minthe must realize that Antheia had a point about her not making the effort to improve her surroundings!

Just then another owl screeched. Oh, wait! It wasn't another owl making that noise—it was Minthe! Persephone put her hands over her ears. Ye gods, what an awful sound!

Reaching out, Minthe grabbed hold of the dog-shaped box and tugged it from Antheia. She tried to open it, but when the lid wouldn't budge for her, she tucked it under one arm. Then, in a fury, she lunged toward Antheia and grabbed her by the ankle.

"Hey! Let go of me!" screamed Antheia. She wiggled her leg and tried to jerk free, but Minthe held on, pulling. Before Persephone could get over her shock and spring into action, the water nymph swiftly dragged Antheia into the river.

"Help!" cried Antheia, her arms flailing. "I can't swim! And even if I could, I wouldn't want to in this river. Yuck!" Her wreath fell from her head to float on the surface of the muddy river. Already sunk to her shoulders now, she tilted her head back to take in gulps of air. She'd go under soon if Persephone didn't act!

All at once Aphrodite's joking words of advice during their conversation about Minthe bubbled up in Persephone's brain: *You can always cast a spell on her and turn her into . . . um . . . a plant or something.*

At the time, Persephone had been quite sure she'd never, ever do any such thing. Now, however, inspired by desperation and Aphrodite's words, she changed her mind. Gazing at Minthe, a spell tumbled from her lips:

"After you set Antheia free,

A naiad you'll no longer be.

The Cocytus you'll no longer tend;

Your water nymph days are at an end.

When I have finished with this chant,

You will transform into a plant!"

As soon as Persephone spoke the last word of her spell, Minthe let go of her captive. The nymph's fingertips began to turn as green as her hair. The green color moved farther, coloring her hands and arms. By the time Persephone waded into the muddy river to rescue Antheia, Minthe's limbs had gone leafy and limp. The green color was slowly overtaking *all* of her.

Persephone grabbed Antheia's wrist with one hand, snagged up her wreath with the other, and towed the girl to shore. There she quickly cast another spell that sucked the muddy water from their skin, clothes, and the wreath, leaving them both clean and dry.

Antheia plopped the wreath atop her head and hugged Persephone in obvious relief. "Thanks so much for the rescue!" Still hugging, they turned together to stare at the muddy water. By this time, Minthe's transformation was nearly complete. She'd become a low-growing, leafy green plant. Though she'd started her transformation in the muddy water, she'd then jumped onto land and begun to spread in all directions, including up to and around the girls' feet.

They hopped about, trying to avoid stepping on her, but in the end they couldn't help it. To their surprise, when they did tromp on her, Minthe's leaves released a sweet smell that was quite pleasing.

"Ooh! Good job. That smell is a humongous improvement," said Antheia.

Persephone nodded. "Yeah, it even masks the stinky sulfur smell."

"So what's the name of this plant you turned her into?" Antheia asked. "I've never seen it before." She bent at the waist to better observe the plant and take a deeper whiff of its delightful fragrance. "Mmm. Nice."

"It's something new," Persephone informed her. Cocking her head, she thought for a few seconds, then added, "I think I'll name it *mint*, in Minthe's honor."

"That's really sweet, considering she wasn't very nice to us," Antheia told her, giving her a quick one-arm hug. "See, I was right when I told that nymph you are cooler and nicer than just about anyone else I know."

"Thanks." Persephone hoped she'd done the right thing, transforming the angry nymph into this new plant. What would Hades say when she told him? He'd understand her need to rescue Antheia. Still, would he be mad at her? He ruled this world, after all, and she had effectively removed the nymph who watched over this river. Hades would have to get someone else to do it now, she supposed. As if he didn't have enough problems to fix around here already!

And what if he also thought she'd acted out of jealousy over Minthe's crush on him? She didn't think jealousy had played a part in her actions, but could she be sure of that? Before Persephone could dwell more on this, Makhai zoomed up to the girls on his winged sandals.

"I went all the way back to the River Styx before I realized you guys weren't behind me," he told them breathlessly. Then he added, "And guess what—Theseus and Pirithous are gone!"

11
The Chair of Forgetfulness

PERSEPHONE AND ANTHEIA QUICKLY UNDID THE laces that bound the wings at their sandals' heels and rose into the air to join Makhai.

"You don't think Theseus and Pirithous disobeyed Hades' signs and ventured into the Underworld somehow, do you?" Antheia asked Makhai as they all flew back toward the River Styx.

"Dunno," said Makhai. "I don't see how they could.

Hades' fence is pretty tall, and they couldn't make their winged sandals fly over it. Not without an immortal's help. Still, I flew all around and called their names over and over. They didn't answer, so . . ."

"We'll find them," Persephone assured him with more certainty than she felt. Secretly, she was mega-worried. If those two boys *had* gotten over Hades' fence somehow, they could be in big trouble. Even if the Furies hadn't already spotted them, there were certain areas of the Underworld that were extremely dangerous, especially for mortals. Poisonous snakes lurked in the frightening Forbidden Meadow, for godness' sake! Or they could accidentally fall into a river of lava in Tartarus and be burned to crisps.

When she, Antheia, and Makhai arrived at the River Styx, at the place where they'd left the two mortal boys, they were surprised to see Hades. He was holding a shovel and staring down at a hole near the fence. His favorite black stallion stood beside him, pawing the ground with a hoof.

He smiled briefly when he saw Persephone approach and then called out to her group. "Something burrowed under my fence! Maybe shrews or moles. Really big ones. There's a hole on the other side, too, so they must've run off into the Underworld. I really don't need those critters in my realm."

As they hovered above the fence, Persephone could see that there was indeed a second hole just a few feet away on the Underworld side of the fence.

"Not critters. *Mortals!*" Makhai exclaimed as he, Antheia, and Persephone all landed to stand beside Hades. "It was Theseus and Pirithous. I don't know how I didn't notice the holes when I was here before, but they must have tunneled under the fence with this shovel."

"*What?* Those mortals dared to ignore the message I created for the scroll-gadgets? Not to mention the signs I posted? Shrews and moles can't read, but what part of 'No Mortals Allowed' did Makhai and Pirithous not understand?" Hades' lips flattened, and a vein pulsed in his throat.

Persephone had rarely seen him so angry before. She wasn't looking forward to telling him what had happened with Minthe when he was in this sort of mood. Not at all. First things first, though: They needed to find those two mortals.

"We told Makhai and Pirithous to wait for us here while we followed the clues to the River Cocytus," she explained quickly. "Guess they didn't." She wondered where the shovel had come from. Maybe some mortal had been using it when he died and still had it in his hand when he arrived to board Charon's ferry. Charon would've made him leave it behind before letting him board to cross the River Styx.

"If they managed to sneak onto Charon's ferry somehow, and cross the Styx after they got under the fence, they could be in the Underworld by now," Antheia said.

Persephone's stomach tightened. "Theseus has coins!" she reminded her teammates.

They looked at her blankly.

"Shades have to pay an obol per passenger. It's the fee to board Charon's ferry," she explained. "The very first time I entered the Underworld by myself, I was able to fool Charon into thinking I was a shade. But he wouldn't have let me onto the boat without an obol, so I had to borrow a coin from a real shade. Theseus could have paid both his fee and Pirithous's with no problem."

Antheia's eyes widened. "Is Charon always so easily fooled by the non-dead?"

Hades shook his head. "No, it's rare. I bet those two did something to distract him so he wouldn't study them too closely." Grimly, he added, "I'd better find them before it's too late. The Underworld and mortals do *not* mix."

"I'll come with you," said Persephone, and he nodded.

"Makhai and I can search too," said Antheia. "If the boys are out in the open, we should be able to spot them from the air."

"But what about the geo-dash?" Makhai protested. "We're ahead in the competition now, but if we wait until we find those mortal boys—if we ever even do—

we'll lose our edge. Maybe I should head back to MOA with our proof while you guys look for them."

Antheia sent him a sharp look. "Who cares about the competition? This is an emergency! We need all of us searching for Theseus and Pirithous."

Makhai opened his mouth as if to argue, then closed it again. "Oh, all right," he grumbled. As he and Antheia winged their way over the fence, Persephone and Hades took off behind them on his black stallion.

After trailing Makhai and Antheia beyond the fence and across the River Styx to the Underworld's entrance, the two pairs of searchers separated. Makhai and Antheia flew leftward—toward the River Cocytus and Tartarus.

Persephone and Hades continued straight ahead. Soon they were flying above several groups of shades at work in the far-flung fields of asphodel. The shades were busy harvesting the roots of the star-shaped white flowers to roast and eat. Not spotting the two boys among the shades, Hades veered his stallion toward a small castle built of black stone and surrounded by a swampy moat. This was his home whenever he wasn't staying over at the Academy.

As they came closer, Persephone peered through the dark mist that swirled around Hades' home, hoping to catch sight of the fugitive mortals. A gloomdial (which worked sort of like a sundial to tell time) stood in the yard near the drawbridge. All along the front of the castle grew dozens of humongous, fragrant, and colorful flowers, which Persephone had planted not long ago. Just as she'd hoped, they really helped to brighten things up.

The petals of the twelve-inch-wide flowers were

yellow in the middle, gradually darkening to orange and then red at the tips. Some of the others had blue petals or even pink and purple ones. These beautiful prickly flowers were the result of a hybrid seed she'd created to celebrate Hades' last birthday. Uniquely suited to the conditions of the Underworld, both the seeds and the flowers could even survive a fire!

"Those two mortals are a lot of trouble," Hades grumbled when they saw no one lurking near the castle. Flying beyond it, they continued rightward toward the desirable neighborhood of the Elysian Fields. As they flew along, their eyes raking the landscape below them, Persephone considered telling Hades about her and Antheia's nearly tragic encounter with Minthe and the spell she had cast on the nymph. But she chickened out—er, *decided to wait*. Because, really, Hades had enough to deal with right now. Plus, she didn't want to worsen his mood!

Just beyond the Elysian Fields, Persephone caught sight of two figures sitting on a bench by the River Lethe, another of the Underworld's five rivers. Its waters were magical and had the power to erase memories. Newly arrived shades were all required to drink from the river in order to forget their earthly lives.

Persephone pointed at the figures. "Hey! Is that Pirithous and Theseus? Yes! There they are!" she called out excitedly, since Hades was looking in the opposite direction.

Hades whipped his head around. "Oh no!" he exclaimed when he saw the two mortal boys. He sounded super alarmed.

Persephone's heart began to beat fast as a thought occurred to her. "Do you think they might have drunk from the river and lost their memories before sitting down to rest?" she asked him worriedly.

"Not sure. But it might not matter. Because that stone bench they're sitting on? It's called the Chair of Forgetfulness for a reason," he told her as his black stallion landed them about thirty feet away from the boys.

They leaped from the horse's back. The two mortal boys continued calmly staring out over the river and seemed not to notice them land.

"Pirithous! Theseus!" Persephone cried out. "Over here!" She waved to attract their attention as she and Hades ran toward the bench.

When both boys finally turned their heads, there was no sign of recognition in their eyes as Hades and Persephone approached. Neither of them made an effort to rise from the bench.

Persephone took in the blank looks on their faces. "Oh no! I'm guessing the Chair of Forgetfulness has similar powers to the River Lethe's waters?" she said to Hades.

"Yeah. And it looks like they've been butt-benched long enough to empty their heads of memories," said Hades. Turned out he was right.

"Who are you?" Theseus asked as they came up to the bench.

Persephone gulped. "You really don't know me? I'm Persephone." She gestured toward Hades. "And this is Hades."

As she introduced the two of them, Pirithous was staring at her as if trying to remember who she was. Now he gave her a goofy smile. "I like you," he said. "You're pretty."

"Um. Thanks?" said Persephone. Apparently

losing his memory hadn't affected his crush on her!

Hades was frowning at Pirithous. Could he be a teeny bit jealous? Persephone wondered. She hoped not. He didn't need to be. That would be silly. But then, hadn't she felt jealous when she'd realized Minthe liked Hades—*a lot*? Strange to think that they were both dealing with unwanted crushes at pretty much the same time. She wondered if Hades had worried about hurting Minthe's feelings or causing embarrassment to them both, just as *she* had with Pirithous.

Theseus and Pirithous twisted their heads to look at each other and then back at Persephone and Hades. "Okay, so we know who you are now, but who are we?" Theseus asked.

"Oh no," Persephone groaned. "And here I'd been worrying they'd lose their memories if they accidentally drank from the River Lethe," she whispered to Hades. "This bench is just as bad! Will their memories return once they get up from it?"

"I don't know," Hades whispered back. "The real problem is going to be getting them *off* the bench."

"Really? Surely they don't like sitting there that much," she replied. She turned back to the boys. While she and Hades had been having their whispered conversation, they'd returned to staring at the river.

"Hey, you guys, if we want to win the geo-dashing competition, we need to get back to Mount Olympus Academy. Let's go!" she called.

The two boys didn't budge. "What's a competition?" Theseus asked, scratching his head in puzzlement.

"And what's a Mount Olympus Academy?" Pirithous asked.

Argh. Just then Hades' stallion, impatient to get moving, stamped the ground and gave a whinny. This gave Persephone an idea. She pointed to the stallion. "Want to go for a horsey ride?" she asked the bench-sitters.

"What's a horsey? What's a ride?" the boys asked. After she explained, they got excited. "Yeah! Horsey ride! Horsey ride!" they chorused.

However, as soon as Theseus and Pirithous tried to stand up from the bench, a serpent shot out from under it. Scaly and purple, it was twice as long as the bench and as big around as a tree trunk! With a hiss, it coiled itself like rope around them and the bench, holding them fast.

Hades caught her astonished eyes and shrugged. "See what I mean? That serpent guards the bench."

"Godsamighty!" Persephone exclaimed in frustration. "Isn't there anything we can do to free them?"

"Maybe," said Hades. He narrowed his eyes at the serpent. "Be gone!" he commanded in a menacing voice. At this, the serpent stuck its head out from under Pirithous's arm and eyed him back, its tongue flicking.

Poof! To her surprise, it disappeared in a puff of black smoke. "Well, that was easy," she said, pleased.

Unfortunately, it became clear that the serpent wasn't the only thing holding the boys to the bench. "Oomph. Umph," they groaned as they attempted to rise. Though they could move their arms and legs, it was as if their rear ends were glued to the bench!

Suddenly Persephone heard the flapping sound of wings overhead. Fearing that the Furies had spied the mortal boys and were coming for them, her heart leaped into her throat. She looked up and then breathed a sigh of relief. It was only Antheia and Makhai.

"Yoo-hoo! Looks like you found them!" Antheia called out as she and Makhai settled to the ground in their winged sandals. "Guess who else just arrived in the Underworld?"

"Team One?" asked Persephone, figuring the brainy Athena's team wouldn't be far behind theirs.

"Bingo!" said Makhai, his voice worried and a little accusing. "We saw them heading for the River Cocytus just a few minutes ago. So if we're still going to win this competition, we need to get a move on!" He waved at the two boys on the bench. "Get up, you troublemakers. C'mon. What's wrong with you? We need to get going."

Theseus and Pirithous stared blankly at Makhai. "Who are you?" Theseus asked. "And what's a troublemaker?" asked Pirithous.

Persephone frowned. "Uh, we have a slight problem." As quickly as possible, she and Hades explained about the Chair of Forgetfulness and how the two mortals from their team were stuck to it.

"Can't we pull them free?" Makhai suggested.

Hades shrugged. "We can try." He didn't sound hopeful, however.

"So, has this happened before to others?" Persephone asked him, not sure she wanted to hear the answer.

He sighed. "Uh-huh."

"What did you do to free them?" asked Antheia.

"Well . . . you're not going to like this . . . ," said Hades. "Before I found all the others, they just sat here so long that they wasted away to dust."

Persephone gasped. "No! We can't let that happen! We've got to figure out a way to save them! Let's try to pull them off."

Makhai and Antheia each took hold of one of Theseus's arms, while Hades and Persephone grabbed Pirithous's. "One, two, three, *pull!*" Makhai shouted. The two goddessgirls and two godboys gritted their teeth and tugged as hard as they could. But the mortal boys' butts barely budged.

"Too bad we're not stronger," said Antheia.

Persephone snapped her fingers. "Hey! That's it! You said Team One is here. Heracles is on that team, and he's *super* strong. I'm sure he'll help. After all, he'll want to rescue his cousin," she said, pointing at Theseus.

Theseus's face lit up in a big smile. "I have a cousin?"

"Yup," said Persephone. The others rolled their eyes.

"What's a cousin?" asked Pirithous. The two mortal boys looked at each other in question, then raised and lowered their shoulders, totally clueless.

"Heracles is mortal, though," Hades reminded Persephone. "No mortals allowed in the Underworld, no exceptions, remember? I hope he obeyed my signs and is waiting on the other side of my fence."

"Can't you please make this one teeny exception for him? It's an emergency," said Persephone.

After gazing for a few seconds at the two boys, whose expressions remained sweetly vacant and goofy, Hades was finally won over. He nodded. "I guess it's okay this one time. But keep watch for the Furies, everybody."

Just as they were discussing who should go fetch Heracles (and the rest of Team One), a boy gave an angry shout from above. They all looked up.

"Hey!" yelled Kydoimos. Purple cloak flapping,

he, Iris, and Ares zoomed down to land among them. "Did you guys steal the container we were supposed to find at the river?" Kydoimos accused.

Persephone and Antheia exchanged a look of startled realization. Ye gods! Minthe had been holding on to the dog-shaped box when Persephone had changed her to mint. That box and its contents must have gotten transformed into mint too. But that explanation could wait until later. Right now there was a more immediate problem to solve. If the Furies got here before Heracles, Theseus and Pirithous really might have to stay butt-benched in the Underworld forever!

12

To the Rescue!

WE DIDN'T STEAL THE CONTAINER," Persephone assured Kydoimos as he and his two teammates laced the wings at their sandals' heels to still them.

Straightening, he scowled at her as if he didn't believe her. "Then where is—"

"Never mind about that right now," she said, interrupting. "We need help!" Quickly, she and her teammates explained about the Chair of Forgetfulness and how Theseus and Pirithous had sneaked under Hades' fence and gotten stuck to it. "Heracles' strength is probably our best bet for freeing them," Persephone breathlessly finished.

"But he and Athena stayed back at the River Styx," Ares said. "On account of Heracles being mortal. Athena decided to keep him company while the rest of us flew to the Cocytus."

Hades looked around the group. "Well? Go get him, someone! Since it's an emergency, I'll allow him to enter the Underworld this once. But we'll all need to keep an eye out for the Furies. If they find out mortals sneaked under my fence into the Underworld, these two boys are toast."

"I can bring Heracles and Athena here in a snap," Iris offered. After speedily conjuring a ball of rainbow magic, she wound up and threw it. *Brrrng!* Instantly a pretty, sparkling rainbow arched from where she stood to a place unseen in the distance, which Persephone guessed must be the far bank of the River Styx. Iris's aim was *that* good. "Back in a jiff," Iris called out. Then she slid up and over the rainbow bridge she'd created and out of sight.

While Iris was fetching Heracles and Athena, Persephone and Antheia finally told the others about their encounter with Minthe. "She was holding on to the box that contained the fourth-clue objects when I transformed her into a plant. Which I had to do to rescue Antheia," Persephone explained when she and Antheia reached that part of their story.

Antheia nodded, and then added, "I'm guessing the box and objects must have become mint too."

Persephone nodded in agreement. She'd been

watching Hades' face while she and Antheia spoke. Most of the way through their story, he'd frowned. Clearly, he was not happy with what had happened. But was he unhappy on their behalf? Or on Minthe's? Or both? Persephone felt a knot in the pit of her stomach. What if he was angry at her for transforming that nymph into a plant? And also for not telling him about it right away? She wished she knew what he was thinking. But she didn't want to ask him with others around.

While listening to the girls' story, Ares had been skipping rocks across the waters of the Lethe. Seemingly mesmerized, Theseus and Pirithous watched his game from the Chair of Forgetfulness. Now Ares stopped throwing rocks and turned toward the girls. "Sorry, but I think our team kind of stomped all over her while we were trying to find the box. Oops."

"That mint stuff you created smelled sweet," Kydoimos added to Persephone. "It really helped mask the nasty sulfur smell."

To her surprise, he smiled at her. Whoa! Had Kydoimos meant his remark as a compliment to her? she wondered. Then again, he might have meant it as an insult to the Underworld and Hades. If so, the insult wouldn't succeed, since Hades thought the Underworld was perfect just the way it was.

And indeed, Hades didn't react to Kydoimos's statement at all. Instead he said, "Whether or not Heracles is able to free Theseus and Pirithous, I'm going to need to get over to the River Cocytus soon." With a sidelong glance at Persephone that she found hard to interpret, he added, "After I restore Minthe to her former self, I'll see what she has to say for herself."

Feeling guilty that her transformation of Minthe had resulted in more work for her crush, Persephone said, "Shall I go with you?"

Hades flashed her a smile. "I'd like that." *Phew,* she thought. He must not be angry with her after all.

Seconds later, Iris, Heracles, and Athena came sliding over the rainbow. As soon as they landed, Heracles sprang into action. "Let's get you off this bench, cuz," he said to Theseus. "And you too," he told Pirithous.

Theseus's face lit up. "*You're* my cousin? Hey! I like that thing you're wearing. What is it?" he added, pointing to Heracles' cape.

"It's my lion cape," Heracles informed him.

"I like it too," said Pirithous. "Can I borrow it sometime?"

"No," Heracles said brusquely.

Persephone and the others quickly formed a semicircle in front of the bench so they'd be ready to help if necessary as Heracles moved to stand behind the two bench-bound boys. He reached under their shoulders and wrapped one of his hugely muscled arms around each boy's waist. "Brace yourselves. I'll try to tug you both loose at the count of three," he told them.

"Okay," they sing-songed calmly.

"They've both lost their memories," Persephone whispered to Athena, who had come to stand beside her. "They probably don't know enough to be afraid that this could hurt."

Athena nodded. "Iris told us. I hope their memories will return once they're off that bench."

"One, two, *three*!" counted Heracles. His feet were planted wide and his muscles tensed as he began to pull. "Umph. Omph," he grunted through gritted teeth.

The others all held their breath as Heracles strained to release Theseus and Pirithous from the bench. If anyone could succeed at the task, it would be this superstar strongboy. According to Athena, who had been with him at the time, Heracles had once uprooted a stand of huge trees with his bare hands and tossed them into a pile to create a dam. And it had cost him very little effort. Still, for a few moments it seemed as if his famed strength would not be enough to free his cousin and Pirithous. But then . . . *Rrrippp!*

All of a sudden Heracles stumbled backward with a boy locked under each arm. Luckily, he managed to catch his balance before all three could tumble to the ground.

"Heracles? What's up?" Theseus asked as his cousin released him and Pirithous.

"I think he's regained his memories," Persephone whispered to Athena, who nodded.

Pirithous rubbed his eyes. Then, noticing that he was being stared at, particularly by Ares and Hades, who were standing slightly in back of him, he asked, "Wha . . . what's going on?"

"Dudes!" Ares said in a rush to both boys. "You might want to cover your backsides. Feeling a bit breezy back there?"

"Huh?" Theseus and Pirithous said at the same time.

"Seems your behinds left something behind!" Grinning, Heracles pointed to the bench, where two big, round patches of cloth that matched the tunics of Theseus and Pirithous remained firmly attached.

As they'd been pried up, the seat of each boy's tunic had ripped off to remain on the bench!

After glancing over their shoulders, the two mortal boys turned a brighter red than Persephone's hair. Meanwhile, the four girls in the group looked at one another and then burst into giggles.

Pirithous scowled at them as he and Theseus hastily tried to pull back the sides of their tunics to cover any bareness. "It's not funny!"

"S'okay, bro," Theseus said to Pirithous good-naturedly. "It actually *is* sort of funny." He glanced over at Hades. "And it's probably what we deserve for disobeying your rules and tunneling into the Underworld."

"Yeah," Hades agreed, chuckling. "It kind of is."

Makhai slipped off his purple cloak and held it out to Theseus. "Here," he said gruffly. "No one wants to see your butt hanging out." He glanced over at Kydoimos. "How about letting Pirithous borrow yours?"

Kydoimos stared at Makhai, a look of surprise on his face. He probably wasn't used to Makhai taking the lead on anything, thought Persephone. Especially to suggest he do something *nice*. Kydoimos's jaw dropped open, but then he closed it. "Oh, all right," he said. He shrugged off his cloak and handed it to Pirithous.

Pirithous smiled at him and whipped it on. "Hey, thanks!"

Kydoimos scowled at him. "Just don't go telling any of your mortal friends that I let you wear it. That'd ruin my reputation!"

Huh? thought Persephone. He *liked* being known as a bully? That was crazy! Athena caught her eye and shrugged. *I know what you're thinking and I agree,* her look seemed to say.

Seconds later a faint screech came from somewhere overhead. Antheia pointed up at the sky. "Whoa! Look at those huge birds winging toward us," she asked. "Oh, wait. Are they—"

"Leaping Olympians!" Persephone interrupted. "The Furies are coming!" Though they were still too far away to see clearly which Fury was which, she could make them out well enough.

"Quick!" Iris shouted. "My rainbow will take the three mortals to safety much faster than winged sandals. In fact, we can *all* slide over it."

Kydoimos frowned. "But our team still needs an object of proof from this location!"

Overhearing, Antheia urged, "No time. We can explain what happened to Muse Urania and ask if

210

we can share our team's fourth object with you guys."

"Sounds good to me," said Athena. She grabbed Heracles' hand and dragged him over to Iris's rainbow. As Antheia started to do the same with Theseus, he called out, "And we can ask her to declare a tie between our two teams."

Kydoimos grunted, seemingly satisfied at this.

Makhai and Pirithous frowned at the idea, but, as they both knew, without Heracles' rescue, Theseus and Pirithous would still be stuck to the Chair of Forgetfulness. Asking Muse Urania to declare a tie was the least their team could do!

Persephone slipped off her backpack and ran over to hand it to Antheia. "All our proof objects and three of our team's scroll-gadgets are inside. Plus a few apples, if you're hungry," she told her teammate. "I'm going to stay behind for a while to help Hades."

"Thanks," Antheia told her. "After our two teams see Muse Urania and give her the proof objects and gadgets, I'll leave your backpack in Aphrodite's room so you can get it from her later." The two gave each other a quick hug before parting.

Pirithous had trailed Theseus and Antheia over to the rainbow. But when he came up to Persephone, he stopped and just stood there gazing at her. "Go!" she urged him, peeking nervously at the fast-approaching Furies. Already Athena, Heracles, Antheia, and Theseus were slipping over Iris's rainbow bridge. For a moment she wondered if Pirithous was afraid of it for some reason.

But then he grinned at her. "I'll go, but only if you change your mind about staying and come with me."

Argh! His crush on her was one memory Persephone had hoped would *not* come back to

 212

him! Seeking support, she glanced over at Hades. However, he gave no sign of having heard Pirithous. His head was tilted back and his gaze was upward as he kept a concerned eye on the approaching Furies. He already had to deal with a nymph turned into a plant and a hole under his fence. Having to face a trio of furious Furies was probably not something he wanted to add to his to-do list right now!

Luckily, Iris came to the rescue. "Come on," she said, tugging on Pirithous's arm. "It's fun. I'll go with you!"

Brightening, Pirithous smiled at Iris and took her hand. "Hey, cool hair! What's your name?" he asked her. As they stepped onto the rainbow and began to slide up and over its arch, he let out a whoop. "This *is* fun!"

Maybe he'd transfer his crush to the goddess of

rainbows, Persephone thought. Though this would be a relief, she'd feel a little sorry for Iris. Because she already had a crush who liked her back—the godboy Zephyr, who controlled the warm west wind of spring. However, Iris would probably be able to handle Pirithous. After all, not so long ago she'd managed to trick and capture a windbag giant named Typhon, who had terrorized and destroyed villages and towns throughout Greece.

Although Ares, Kydoimos, and Makhai didn't need to rush off—they were godboys, not mortals subject to the Furies' wrath—they soon followed the others over the rainbow bridge. When it vanished, Persephone knew that her three teammates, plus all of Team One, must've landed safely on the far side of the River Styx. They were out of the Underworld.

"That was close," said Hades, heaving out a

relieved breath. They both gazed upward. The Furies had changed course. Instead of continuing toward her and Hades, they were now doubling back the way they'd come.

"Do you think they saw Theseus and Pirithous, or they just suspected mortals were somewhere around here?" Persephone asked Hades as the two of them climbed onto the back of his black stallion.

"Hard to say. I'm just glad it's over. Now on to the next problem." He patted his horse's neck. "To the River Cocytus!" he called.

Persephone held on to Hades, clasping her hands around his waist, as his stallion soared into the air. He was silent during the journey, and as they drew closer to the river, Persephone began to wonder again if he might be upset with her—even just a little bit—for transforming Minthe.

Finally she blurted out, "I didn't change Minthe into a plant because she was crushing on you!"

Hades whipped his head around to look back at her. "Huh? You thought she was crushing on me? Why would you think . . . oh, wait . . ." He wrinkled his brow, looking thoughtful. "So *that's* why she's been acting so needy lately. Well, even if you're right about that crush, I know you'd never have transformed her if you hadn't been truly worried about Antheia's safety."

Persephone smiled at him. She felt grateful that he accepted without doubt her explanation for why she'd changed Minthe. Because if she was being honest, there was a teensy little part of her that still wondered if her motives had been completely pure.

She also felt oddly grateful that Hades hadn't even realized that Minthe *like*-liked him. As Aphrodite often said, boys could be pretty clueless when it came to how girls felt about them. Despite girls leaving plenty of hints!

All too soon, the black stallion landed them beside the River Cocytus. "Wow, your new plant is *hot*!" said Hades the moment he dismounted. He shot her a smile as he used his new word for "cool."

Persephone smiled back, glad that in a day full of difficulties his mood seemed to have actually lightened. And, as Kydoimos had said, the sweet smell of the mint really did mask the stinky sulfur. It was yet another thing to be grateful for, she thought. Without actually meaning to, she'd been able to use her talents as the goddess of growing things to create a plant with true usefulness!

Because he was godboy of the Underworld, Hades had no trouble extracting Minthe from the large patch of mint, despite Persephone's earlier spell. He simply commanded, "Minthe, arise!"

At once the beautiful green-haired nymph rose up from the mint. "You!" she spat out, the moment she saw Persephone. "Look at what you've done. My hair! It's all matted now. And I've got the worst headache from being stomped on!" She held up one of her arms. "See this bruise?" she said, pointing to a small purple spot on the inside of one of her forearms. "It's all your fault," she complained. "I don't know why you had to go cast a spell on—"

"Stop!" Hades commanded, holding up a hand. Looking sternly at Minthe, he said, "I believe you owe Persephone an apology for trying to drown her friend."

Minthe crossed her arms. Glowering at Persephone, she said, "If anyone should apologize, it should be her!"

Persephone couldn't believe it! It would feel so great to put this lesser goddess in her place! She opened her mouth to do so, but then closed it. Because she had noticed that Minthe's lower lip had begun to quiver. Was she about to cry?

Something shifted inside Persephone. Instead of seeing what she expected to see—a spiteful, angry, uppity nymph—she looked beyond Minthe's glowering gaze and saw the fear and misery shimmering within the nymph's dark eyes.

She considered how it must feel to be Minthe. Humiliated in front of the very boy she was crushing on. Bound to the sluggish and horrible River Cocytus day in and day out. Lonely.

Was Hades seeing what she was seeing? Persephone wondered as she looked steadily into Minthe's eyes. Maybe. Or maybe he was simply remembering what Persephone had said about the nymph crushing on him. Whatever the reason, his voice softened as he said to the girl, "I'm afraid that after this I can't let you go back to caring for the Cocytus."

There was no way Persephone could miss the flash of happy hope in Minthe's eyes upon hearing this. But that glint of hope soon turned to despair when Hades added, "I'll transfer you to one of the other five rivers of the Underworld. Maybe the Acheron. Or Phlegethon." At this, Minthe drooped.

The Acheron, known as the River of Woe, would hardly be a step up from the Cocytus, thought Persephone. Nor would the Phlegethon, a terrifying river of fire that flowed in the depths of Tartarus. Compared to her and her MOA friends, it didn't seem like poor Minthe had much in her life to be grateful for. No wonder the nymph was so unhappy. (Not that unhappiness was any excuse for bad behavior, of course, but it certainly made it more understandable!)

As Hades began to debate aloud the merits of the Acheron versus the Phlegethon, Persephone got an idea. "Hold on a minute," she said, interrupting him. "Can I ask Minthe something?"

"Yeah . . . sure," he said.

Persephone looked deeply into Minthe's eyes. "If you could live wherever you wanted to, where would that be?" she asked gently.

13
Mealtime at MOA

So WHAT DID I MISS OUT ON AFTER YOU GOT back?" Persephone asked Athena as she plopped down her tray and joined her friends at their usual table in MOA's cafeteria that evening.

She and Hades had arrived at the Academy on his stallion an hour or so after the others. Once they'd arrived, they'd needed to make a stop on the grounds near the sports fields before going into the Academy's main building. And then, alone, she'd stopped by the cafeteria kitchen just as a huge thunderstorm had begun. *Boom! Boom!* Through a window she'd seen flashes of lightning slice the sky. *Uh-oh,* she'd thought. *Zeus must be throwing thunderbolts around.* He only did that when he was very angry about something, and she'd wondered what it could be.

Before leaving the Underworld, she'd realized that the mint she'd created was an herb, and therefore edible. So she'd pulled up some of it to take to a fellow student named Hestia. She was goddessgirl of the hearth and a talented cook. In fact, she worked in the kitchen during her spare time, creating new dishes, and Persephone and her friends had once taken a cooking class from her.

Hestia had been thrilled to receive the new herb from her only minutes ago. "Mm-mm," she'd said, inhaling the mint deeply. "What a delicious scent! Thank you sooo much. I can't wait to experiment with this. It'll be perfect to flavor both savory *and* sweet dishes!"

Now, reunited at dinner with her BFFs, Persephone watched Athena trade looks with both Artemis and Aphrodite. "Well . . . ," Athena began uncertainly.

Although neither Artemis nor Aphrodite took Science-ology and they hadn't gone geo-dashing, they obviously knew whatever Athena was about to say, Persephone realized. "Okay. Out with it," she said. "Did Muse Urania declare a tie between our two teams?"

Athena set down her fork. "Actually, she decided not to pick a winner at all. She said she'll save the trophies for another contest later this year."

Persephone swallowed the sip of nectar she'd just taken and raised an eyebrow in surprise. "Huh? Why?"

Truthfully, she'd almost forgotten about the trophies. Not that it wouldn't have been nice to receive one. But after all that had happened that day, winning a trophy just didn't seem that important anymore.

"Because there were some, er, irregularities and cheating," Athena told her. She squirmed in her chair, looking uncomfortable.

"But it wasn't my fault Minthe was holding the box when she dragged Antheia into the river," Persephone protested. She speared a piece of tomato from her celestial salad.

Athena shook her head. "Muse Urania didn't blame you for that irregularity. It was the cheating by that tech genius Pirithous that was the problem."

"*He* cheated?" Persephone echoed, confused. "I know Makhai tried to, but he wasn't able to make it happen."

Artemis had leaned down under the table to feed her dogs bites of her dinner. Now she popped back up. "Well, Pirithous *did* make it happen. That boy genius discovered a way to hack all the scroll-gadgets," she told Persephone. "He changed messages to lead the other six teams astray."

"Huh? Changed them in what way?" Persephone asked.

Aphrodite swallowed a bite of yambrosia stew. "He deleted letters and words in the second clue and planted a bogus message to mislead other teams about where to go."

While Persephone had been talking to Artemis and Aphrodite, Athena had taken a piece of papyrus from her scrollbook bag and scribbled something down on it. Now she showed Persephone what she'd written, saying, "This was the second clue all the teams were supposed to get."

Persephone read the clue aloud: "'We love frolicking in waves and sunning ourselves on beaches. To see us is an omen of good fortune. Our image is even on a coin! Can you find us?'"

"Yes, I remember that one," she said. "You mean it's not the same clue the rest of you got?"

Athena shook her head. "Not at all. I'll show you what all the other teams got instead." Leaning over the piece of papyrus, she quickly crossed out letters and words, so that now the clue was much shorter and read: *We love licking ourselves. Our image is even on a coin! Can you find us?*

Persephone's jaw dropped. "If I read that, I'd think of cats!"

"Or a member of the cat *family*, right?" said Athena. "When we asked Archimedes, our team's scroll-gadget scientist, about coins with engravings of cats on them, he told us about a tetrobol with a picture of a lion on it."

As everyone knew, a tetrobol was a coin worth four obols.

"Wasn't Archimedes that mathematician who made some important discovery while he was taking a bath?" Aphrodite asked, flipping a length of her golden hair over one shoulder.

Athena nodded. "Yes! The story goes that one day when he got into the tub, he noticed that the further he sank down, the higher the water rose and the more it spilled out. It dawned on him that the volume of water displaced by his body had to be equal to the volume of the part of his body underwater. This led to Archimedes' principle, which explains why objects sink or float."

"Interesting," said Persephone. No surprise that

her brainy friend would know that story! "But back to the cat family . . ."

"Oh, right. Sorry," said Athena. "Got off on a *tangent* there." She laughed. "Get it? A tangent can mean a completely different train of thought. But it's also a geometrical concept—a line that touches a circle or ellipse at just one point."

It took some effort for Persephone not to roll her eyes. Sometimes Athena was too smart for her own good! "So I'm guessing every team except mine went to look for lions in Africa?" she asked.

Athena nodded. "You got it!"

"That Pirithous!" Persephone huffed. "I wondered why he kept fiddling with his scroll-gadget. And why we hardly ever saw the other teams. I mean, I knew he was supposed to be good at tech stuff, but I had no idea—"

"Nobody else did either," Athena said. "My team was misled by that false clue, but only for a while. I got super suspicious when we got another message soon afterward. Because though Archimedes delivered it, his voice sounded different from before."

"Different how?" Persephone asked.

"I wasn't sure at the time," Athena told her. "But now I think maybe it was Pirithous's voice. It said, 'Urgent message: Competition canceled. Please return to Science-ology class immediately!'"

Persephone remembered Pirithous, out of range of the others, speaking to his scroll-gadget and tapping furiously on its keys back on Mount Cyllene. That was just after her team had received the second geo-dash clue, but before Athena's team had gotten it. She'd assumed Pirithous had been asking the head of Theophrastus questions to help their team figure out the clue, but now it appeared he'd been recording his misleading clue and "urgent" message.

"He may be a genius, but he wasn't smart about what he did, because obviously the teacher figured out something went wrong when the teams reported what had happened," said Aphrodite. At least that's what Ares told me. Pheme got wind of the news after we got back—she has her ways. Now everybody's talking about it." Pheme was the goddessgirl of gossip and could spread news, good or bad, faster than anyone they knew.

Persephone had been sipping from her carton of nectar, but now she set it down with a thump. Some of the nectar spilled onto the table. After wiping up the splash, she glanced around the cafeteria. "I'd like to give that crafty mortal boy a piece of my mind!" she exclaimed. "Too bad I don't see him anywhere."

Aphrodite pushed back a lock of golden hair that had fallen over her shoulder. "I'm pretty sure he and Theseus have already left MOA," she told Persephone.

"They were in kind of a hurry," Artemis added with a grin. "Principal Zeus wasn't happy when he found out what Pirithous had done. After all, the scroll-gadgets were *Zeus's* invention. He didn't like that they'd been messed with."

Athena nodded. "Yeah, Dad was more furious than the Furies! You know what he's like when he's angry. I'm sure everyone noticed all the noise he was making up in the heavens."

Persephone blinked. "I guess that explains the thunderstorm I heard a little while ago! Maybe he should've aimed a bolt at Pirithous," she grumbled. "Just a small zap that would make him think twice the next time he thought about cheating during a competition!"

Her friends laughed so hard that Artemis snorted some nectar out of her nose.

When they calmed down, Persephone added, "Not that I wish him *real* harm. But he should count himself lucky he's gone. Because he would not have liked the tongue-lashing I would have given him!" Then she thought of something. "Was Theseus involved in the cheating too?" she asked. She hoped not. He was Heracles' cousin, after all.

Athena shook her head. "Heracles said Theseus told him he didn't know Pirithous had been cheating and actually felt bad for having invited him along. And for letting Pirithous talk him into sneaking into the Underworld."

Persephone nodded. "Figures that was Pirithous's

idea. It was a dumb thing to do. Maybe even dumber than the cheating. If Heracles hadn't helped to free them, they could've been stuck there forever."

As angry as she was with Pirithous, Persephone was surprised to find herself feeling a bit sorry for him too. Yes, he'd acted rashly and foolishly. His mess-ups were numerous. He'd hacked the scroll-gadgets to cheat, let go of her hand while flying—on purpose, she was sure now—and sneaked into the Underworld. But despite all his faults, she'd enjoyed his enthusiasm for flying, and she could appreciate his genius in rigging the competition in his favor, even though that was a misguided thing to do.

People were never all good or all bad, and if you thought hard enough about it, you could usually figure out what was behind even their worst behavior, she reflected. Perhaps Pirithous's seeming need to win at all costs sprang from a desire to feel important and impress others. Whatever. She hoped Theseus wouldn't be *too* hard on his friend.

On the other hand, she thought, Pirithous had gotten off pretty easily. She doubted very much that he'd ever be allowed to visit Mount Olympus Academy again, however. Maybe that was punishment enough? And the fact that he hadn't succeeded in winning a trophy after all? She supposed it was too much to hope that the mortal boy had learned a lasting lesson. Time would tell.

Having finished eating, Aphrodite touched her napkin to her mouth. "So what happened with Minthe?" she asked Persephone. "Athena told us you changed her into a groundcover plant called mint to rescue Antheia from her clutches?"

Persephone scraped up one last spoonful of

ambrosia pudding. "Yeah! That plant is awesome. Minthe's back to being herself, though. C'mon. I'll show you." She picked up her empty tray and headed for the tray return.

"Huh?" said Aphrodite. But she, Athena, and Artemis picked up their trays too, and followed. As they were putting their trays in the return, Persephone glanced toward Athena. "I'm confused about something. If Pirithous changed the second clue and then sent a false message to make teams return to the Academy, how did you figure out the true clues?"

"I was wondering about that too," said Aphrodite.

Artemis nodded. "Likewise."

"Well, as it turned out, we had two lucky breaks," Athena said as the girls left the cafeteria. "The first was running into members of Team Two."

"My brother was on that team," Artemis remarked before Athena could go on. Her three dogs, Amby, a beagle, Nectar, a greyhound, and Suez, a bloodhound, had followed the girls out of the cafeteria. Now the dogs bounded ahead as Persephone led everyone to the entrance of the Academy and pushed through the doors to the outside.

"Yes, I know," Athena told Artemis. She turned toward Persephone. "It was Apollo who told me he'd seen your team in a particular spot near some monk seals on the coast of the Aegean. He thought your team must have gotten clue number two really wrong. But because the message to return to the Academy had made me suspicious, I talked my team into flying to that spot anyway." She paused. "Can you guess what we found there?"

Persephone nodded. "A large pink clamshell container with monk-seal figures in it."

"Well, yes, that too," Athena agreed. "But near the container we also found a scroll-gadget that some-one from your team had accidentally left behind."

Persephone's eyes widened. "Antheia's! She thought it might've fallen into the Aegean after we left the beach. I guess it must have dropped out of her pocket just *before* we left, though."

"Hey, where are we going?" Aphrodite inter-rupted to ask as Persephone led them all down the granite steps to the marble courtyard.

"You'll see," Persephone said with a grin.

"So, to make a long story short," Athena went on, as the girls and the dogs followed Persephone across the now thunderless, sunny courtyard, "we followed the clues on the dropped scroll-gadget till we caught up with you in the Underworld. I, or one of my team members, probably would've told you and your team about the scroll-gadget then," she added, "but right away we had bigger things to worry about."

Persephone nodded before starting over a grassy lawn that sloped downward toward the sports fields. "Bigger things named Pirithous and Theseus and the Furies, you mean?"

"You got it," said Athena. "Antheia told me about losing her scroll-gadget on our way back to the Academy," she added. "She was worried my dad would be angry she'd lost it, so she was relieved when I told her my team had found it and I returned it to her."

"Oh, good," said Persephone. She really liked Antheia, and their near-tragic experience with Minthe had made her feel an even stronger friendship toward the goddessgirl. She was glad none of Zeus's anger had been toward Antheia.

Halfway to the fields the four goddessgirls came to a stone fountain that Poseidon had designed in the shape of a big O for the Olympic Games a while back. At its center, water sprayed outward in loops and twists from the fountain's many spigots. The water seemed to dance in the air for a few seconds before tumbling back into a mosaic-tiled pool below. That was new, thought Persephone. The waters hadn't danced before. Come to think of it, the fountain's waters looked bluer and cleaner, as did its mosaic tiles.

When she stopped in front of the fountain, her BFFs did too. Gazing into the water, she called out, "Hey, Minthe! Come out and meet my friends!"

Instantly, the beautiful green-haired water nymph materialized in the pool at the bottom of the fountain. With a graceful movement she rose to stand and extended her hands toward the girls.

"Hi. Nice to meet you all. Welcome to my fountain." There was a joyful sparkle in her dark eyes as she said to Persephone, "I absolutely love it here! Thank you for convincing Zeus to let me come live at MOA. Did you notice the new pattern of the dancing waters? My idea!"

"You did that? It's awesome," said Persephone. "And you've spruced things up. This fountain has never looked better."

"Thanks," Minthe replied almost shyly. "My river was too overwhelming for me—so big and dirty. I didn't know how to even begin to take care of it. But this fountain is beautiful and will be a cinch to keep clean. I've got more ideas for new water dances and mosaic decorations too!"

When Minthe had named MOA as the place she'd most want to live, Persephone had immediately thought of this fountain. It was the perfect home for the nymph. Luckily, Hades had agreed to let the nymph leave the Underworld. And after a quick exchange of magic-breeze messages, he and Persephone had gotten permission from Zeus and Poseidon for Minthe to live in the fountain.

From within its shallow waters Minthe could see students walking to and fro from the Academy to the sports fields and the gymnasium. She could watch them playing ball games on the lawn. And she could chat with and get to know those who often perched on the edge of the stone fountain's pool to rest and relax. Which was what Persephone and her friends did now.

As they struck up a conversation with Minthe about the various students and teachers and classes at MOA, a ball suddenly splash-landed in the pool. Kydoimos raced over to the base of the fountain. "Oops. Sorry Minthe!" Ignoring the other girls, he grinned at the nymph. "You'd think my aim would get better, but I just keep chucking that ball in."

"No problem, Ky," Minthe replied, fishing it out.

Ky? The other girls exchanged amused looks. Persephone waited for Kydoimos to get mad and make some snarky comment. But he actually seemed pleased with the nickname Minthe had given him. Smiling back at the godboy, the nymph held the ball out to him. His hand brushed hers when he took it from her, and they both blushed. "Later, then," said "Ky" before running off.

"You do know his aim is just fine, right?" Aphrodite said to Minthe when Kydoimos was out of earshot.

"Yeah," said Artemis, "He's tossing that ball into your fountain on purpose."

"Because he's crushing on you," said Athena, as if to make things perfectly clear.

Minthe blushed again. "Do you really think so?"

Aphrodite arched an eyebrow at the nymph. "Trust me, as the goddessgirl of love I've got a sixth sense about these things."

Minthe sighed dreamily. "Awesome. I think Ky's sweet."

Artemis was sitting next to Persephone. Leaning forward, she whispered in her ear, "Minthe may well be the first girl to ever think that about Kydoimos in the history of the world."

Persephone had to stifle a giggle. To tell the truth, she'd been a bit worried that Minthe's crush on Hades might continue to be a problem, since she'd probably see him just as much here at MOA as she did in the Underworld. But now it seemed that she'd transferred her crush to Kydoimos, who luckily returned her affection!

As the other girls continued to chat, Persephone became lost in reflection. She was pleased with herself for learning to see beyond the expected. Not only when it came to the existence of white blackbirds (she couldn't wait to ask Muse Urania if Pausanias had seen what *he* expected to see when he'd almost certainly identified a snow finch as a white blackbird), but in people's actions and behavior, too. It was a real skill!

Other people's behavior—not just Minthe's, Makhai's, Kydoimos's and Pirithous's—was much less puzzling (or aggravating!) when, instead of judging them, you tried to put yourself in their sandals and think how you might feel in their place.

Feeling the warm sun on her back, Persephone trailed a hand in the cool waters of the fountain's pool. A group of giggling girls who were walking toward the sports fields had begun to turn cartwheels across the lawn. One of them was Antheia. She did a double take when she caught sight on Minthe in the fountain, but then she saw Persephone and smiled and waved.

Knowing Antheia, she'd be quick to forgive Minthe for what had happened back at the River Cocytus. In fact, maybe she already had. Persephone smiled and waved back at the girl, feeling truly grateful for all she had—her friends, her school, her immortality, and . . . well . . . everything!